NEVER SAY GOODBYE

Suzanne McMinn

A KISMET® Romance

METEOR PUBLISHING CORPORATION
Bensalem, Pennsylvania

First Printing May 1993.

ISBN: 1-56597-065-9

Printed in the United States of America.

For my supportive-beyond-the-call-of-duty husband, Gerald, who always believes in me and helps me make all my dreams come true. Thanks for reading and editing every word when you really wanted to watch sports on TV instead.

SUZANNE McMINN

Suzanne McMinn lives by the lake in Granbury, Texas, the real-life inspiration for the fictional Granbury, Georgia, of *Never Say Goodbye*. She knew she wanted to be a writer by age five and set her sights on romance novels when she was twelve. Now she fulfills her dream of writing while enjoying her wonderful husband, two young children and three cranky cats.

ONE

Felicia Marick's arms ached with the strain of drawing the paddle through the cool water of Lake Granbury. She'd forgotten how tiring it could be to paddle a canoe alone, and she regretted the impulsive early-morning excursion. She'd almost dropped the paddle several times. The dawn air chilled her fingers, stiffening her grip.

She shouldn't have gone so far up the cove, she thought numbly, but the serenity of the lake at dawn had seduced her. She'd been tempted by memories of long-ago mornings spent rowing on the lake, surrounded by water and peace and the soft rustlings of nature.

But she hadn't realized she'd be so exhausted before she returned. She wasn't in shape for rowing these days. It had been eight years since she'd last held an oar. She couldn't just pick up canoeing again that easily.

And she couldn't just pick up her life here in Georgia again that easily.

The light breeze, carrying her so easily on her way out, worked against her now. The muscles in her arms burned as she pushed the oar through the water.

The outline of the old wooden dock loomed up darkly in the misty dawn.

Almost there, she thought. *Won't do this again.*

Then she dropped the paddle.

Felicia reached back to grab it, but it drifted away from her. The canoe bobbed lazily in the opposite direction from the dock.

She reached again. This time she could feel her fingertips barely brushing the end of the paddle. She stretched farther, feeling the strain in her shoulder joint.

Cool water rushed over her body as the canoe flipped, nearly landing on top of her. She gulped for air, spitting water from her mouth as she floundered, slapping her arms around frantically.

The canoe. Where was the canoe?

She swung about searching for it, and spotted it floating toward a stand of dead trees in the middle of the cove. It was closer to her than the dock or shore, so she tried to move toward it, but her sweater, jeans, and tennis shoes felt like lead weights on her limbs. Her arms were already exhausted, and the more she flapped them through the water, the more hopeless the effort seemed as her clothing pulled her under.

Her head sank beneath the lake and she rose up tiredly, spitting another mouthful of water. How could she have forgotten something as basic as a life jacket? The question pounded in her brain, followed by another, more haunting question.

Who would take care of Robin if she drowned? She couldn't let Robin grow up without parents, like she had.

The image of Robin's hazel eyes seared her heart,

energizing her efforts to reach safety. She tried desperately to kick off her tennis shoes and peel the sticky sweater from her arms, but struggling to remove the clothing only forced her under again. She threw her head up and back, gulping for air.

She was so tired. But the persistent memory of Robin's face kept her kicking wearily, shifting her weighted arms through the water. If she could just reach the canoe. . . .

She was buoyed up suddenly by strong thick arms that reached around her waist, pulling her tightly against a warm bare chest.

"You're okay," a deep voice said softly in her ear. "You're going to be okay. I have you."

The voice keyed a strange echo in her memory, but she was too worn out to think of anything else except that she was going to make it. She'd been saved. She would see Robin again. Robin wouldn't grow up unwanted.

Her rescuer pulled her along beside him to the shore. Lifting her out of the water as if she were weightless, he set her gently onto the dewy grass. Grateful for the solid ground beneath her back, Felicia closed her eyes, breathing raggedly.

"Are you okay? Do you need a doctor?" the man asked, his voice concerned.

That voice. She knew that voice.

Felicia opened her eyes. A dark-haired man knelt beside her, his long, lean face peering over hers with vivid, unforgettable blue eyes.

Blue eyes Felicia had not forgotten.

"Brandon Donnelly?" she questioned feebly, her voice cracking.

His eyes flickered.

"Well, if it isn't Felicia Marick," he said, his voice

gaining a sarcastic edge. "I thought it looked like you, but lying there like a drowned rat and all, I couldn't be sure. I never thought I'd see you here again. Silly me to have given up after only eight years. Do you have an answer for my marriage proposal yet?"

Felicia's sea-green eyes widened as she stared up at Brandon speechlessly. Then she began to cough harshly, and she leaned over to her side as she gasped for breath.

She heard Brandon mutter a few colorful words under his breath, then he reached under her back and effortlessly scooped her up into his arms.

She closed her eyes as he carried her, half from exhaustion and half from the need to absorb the shock of his presence. Brandon Donnelly? Last she'd heard, he'd been in New York. She knew his parents had moved away from Granbury, and she'd assumed they'd sold the house they owned next door to her grandmother's old home.

Yet here he was. Larger than life.

Opening her eyes to narrow slits, she took in the bare chest, lightly sprinkled with fine, dark hair. Moving up, she observed the square, firm jaw, wide mouth, and straight nose. She lowered her lashes again, avoiding his eyes.

"Better be unlocked," he said, roughly shifting her weight to one arm as he mounted the steps to her back porch and reached for the door. He jiggled the knob.

"You have to push—" Felicia started.

"I remember."

Brandon threw his weight against the door heavily, swinging Felicia with him.

"Ouch! Put me down," she ordered.

"Fine." He dumped her unceremoniously onto the nearest chair, a recliner that had been casually draped with a dustcover by the realtor after the last tenant's departure. "I guess I just should have left you out there."

"That would have been fine with me," she returned, a shade of anger entering her voice. She raised her hand to touch the tenderness that radiated from her shoulder where she'd hit the door. "I didn't need your help," she lied.

"Right," he said. "You don't need anyone. You can make it on your own. I remember all that."

She stared up at Brandon, her heart pounding. He hadn't changed a bit in eight years, she thought. Well, maybe those tiny lines fanning out from around his eyes hadn't been there, along with the laugh lines framing his mouth. But he was the same Brandon, handsome enough to unnerve a nun and stubborn enough to frustrate a saint.

And Felicia was neither, and never had been.

Then it suddenly registered with her disoriented mind what Brandon was wearing. Or, rather, what he wasn't wearing.

He stood, dripping onto her grandmother's hardwood floor, in nothing but a pair of white underwear that stuck to his body like a second skin. She had to force her gaze away from the swell of manhood beneath the cotton, her eyes traveling instead up and down the rest of his body in a disconnected, nervous appraisal. The years had taken nothing away from the athleticism of his younger days, from his long, muscled legs to his slim, hard torso. She came at last to his face, her cheeks reddening as she met his eyes.

Brandon crossed his arms, watching her, seemingly unembarrassed by either his appearance or her perusal.

"What are you doing?" she sputtered out at last. "How dare you—"

"I guess you wanted me to jump in after you with

all my clothes on?" he questioned calmly. "Then we could have both drowned."

Felicia glared at him. He exuded the same infuriatingly self-confident attitude that he'd always had. It was a facet of his personality that had both attracted and overwhelmed her.

"It's not like it's anything you haven't seen before," Brandon added smoothly.

The memories of their past together pulsated between them. Felicia looked away, lips pursed.

"Just leave, please," she said coolly. "Thank you for rescuing me, if that's what you're waiting for." She sighed. She wasn't ready for this. She hadn't been prepared to see Brandon. "I can't believe this. I can't believe you're the first person I see when I come back to this town."

"We're neighbors, honey. What did you expect?"

"I heard your family moved away," she countered, deciding to ignore the sarcastic endearment.

She remembered her grandmother's telling her that the Donnellys had left Granbury. That was after her grandmother had moved out to California to be with Felicia. She'd been tired and old, and she wasn't with Felicia long before she died.

"They did," Brandon said. "My parents moved to Savannah to be by Joanie and the kids." He quirked an eyebrow at Felicia. "I guess they gave up on me ever delivering some grandkids."

Kids. He used to tell her how he wanted five of them. All boys. Maybe that was part of what had scared her off, she thought. Men, children, small towns, commitment. None of them had ever been Felicia Marick's strong suit.

"What about you?" she asked abruptly, determined

to shut off the train of thought her mind seemed intent on following. "I thought you were in New York."

He lifted a brow cockily.

"Been following my career?" he asked.

Felicia's chest tightened. Yes, she answered internally. She'd taken care to read every review. Brandon's off-Broadway musical-theater career had held a haunting fascination for her. Eight years ago, he'd looked no further ahead than performing at the Granbury Opera House. That hadn't been enough for Felicia. She'd wanted Hollywood, the movies, stardom. She'd tried to talk Brandon into leaving their hometown, for the sake of both of their careers. He wouldn't go with her when she'd asked him. Instead, he'd asked her to stay in Granbury. He'd asked her to marry him.

And Felicia had left him. She'd often wondered what had changed his mind after she'd gone, made him leave Granbury to try his luck in New York City.

Her eyes flickered up to Brandon's, meeting his curious gaze, then she glanced away. No, she wouldn't tell him about the trip she'd made to New York especially to see him in his first popular show, of how she'd wanted to go backstage afterward but had lost her nerve.

"Of course I haven't been following your career," she told him instead. "But, naturally, I've heard of your successes." She hesitated awkwardly. "You never answered my original question. What are you doing in Granbury?"

"My parents keep the house here for vacations," he said with a nonchalant shrug. "I use it now and then."

And he had to be using it now, Felicia thought with a bitter clenching of her stomach. She tried to stand up, lifting herself out of the easy chair with care. Her arms felt sore already, and her legs still moved like they had weights attached. Her knees crumpled, and she grabbed at the side of the chair.

Brandon reached out, tugging her up against his chest. He felt warm, comfortable, and oddly familiar.

Eight years. The words flashed into her head. You shouldn't remember someone so well after eight years.

"Sit down," he growled, pushing her away, forcing her back into the chair.

"I'm okay," she protested, albeit in a feeble voice.

Brandon ignored her. He turned and strode down the hall. Felicia heard the bathroom cabinet open and shut. A moment later, he emerged wearing a forest-green towel knotted around his waist. He carried a thick patchwork quilt, which he thrust at Felicia.

"You look cold," he said. "You got coffee in this place?" He jerked his head in the direction of the kitchen.

"I just got here last night," Felicia said. "Of course not."

"Wait right there. I'll get you some." He headed to the door.

"You don't have to—" Felicia broke off as the back door slammed behind Brandon.

She sighed and pulled the quilt up around her, tugging it protectively up to her neck.

Brandon Donnelly. He was in Granbury.

The memories rushed forth on her, tumbling about in the confusion of feelings her return to her hometown had sparked within her since she had arrived the night before.

Marry me, Felicia. Marry me and stay here with me in Granbury. Brandon's words echoed from the past. His intensity had frightened the then eighteen-year-old Felicia. She hadn't wanted to stay in the small Georgia town where she'd never felt like she belonged. She had wanted out. She had needed to make it on her own, to prove that she could be somebody. Life had taught her the hard way that she couldn't depend on anyone but herself.

And she'd taken the coward's way out. She'd left without saying goodbye.

She jerked out of her reverie as Brandon grunted against the reluctant back door, swinging in with a jar of instant coffee. He dropped the green towel over the back of the couch, having pulled on a pair of faded blue jeans and a white T-shirt. His breath came quickly, and she guessed he'd run all the way to his neighboring house and back.

"You don't have to do this," Felicia said.

I don't want you to do this, she wanted to say. *I don't want you back in my life. I don't want any man in my life.*

Brandon stopped on his way to the kitchen and turned to Felicia. His cobalt-blue eyes met hers.

"I know," he said, and turned away.

When he'd disappeared into the kitchen, Felicia tried standing again. This time her legs worked, a bit rubberlike, but serviceable. She made her way down the hall to the only first-floor bedroom and switched on the lamp. Her suitcase still rested on the floor beside the bed, where she'd dropped it at midnight last night when she'd arrived.

Shutting the door behind her, she kicked off her soaked shoes and peeled off her damp clothes before rummaging through her suitcase. She pulled out a thick terry-cloth robe and lacy underthings. She felt dirty from the lake water. A shower sounded perfect.

Maybe he'll just go away if I stay gone long enough, she thought wearily. She didn't want to deal with Brandon today. A nervous tremble fingered through her veins as she thought of him. A man like Brandon could make you lose sight of the important things in life, Felicia thought. Important things like achieving goals and success. Things that mattered and lasted. Unlike love.

But still, after all these years, Brandon Donnelly could make her heart pound. She frowned in frustration.

How dare he show up in Granbury at the same time she was here?

On that irritated, irrational thought, she slammed down the lid to her suitcase and headed for the bathroom.

This was no way to start her first day in Granbury, she thought. Half drowning in the lake and being rescued by the last person she wanted to see in this town hadn't been tops on her list of things to do first off. She needed all her strength about her today.

In a few short hours she was scheduled to check in at the Granbury Opera House. Felicia had agreed to come home to Granbury, for the first time in eight years, to headline a three-week benefit musical to reopen the Opera House. Once the cultural heartbeat of Granbury, the theater had faltered after the death of its longtime director. Lack of leadership had led to disarray, and the theater had closed after losing much of its financial backing.

The Opera House had served as a magnet to tourists for years. Felicia had gotten her start on that venerated old stage. A start she'd shared with Brandon.

And she'd always known she'd leave someday. She didn't belong in Granbury. She wasn't sure where she belonged, but she was determined to find out.

Felicia twisted on the shower nozzle and leaned her face up into the warm spray, washing away the lake water. At least in L.A., no one cared that Felicia's father, an ex-con who had never married her mother, had run away before she was born, or that her mother had abandoned her illegitimate five-year-old daughter to the care of her aging grandmother.

All they'd cared about was that Felicia had a face and body that photographed "with the perfection of classic art," as one critic had raved. She'd won several roles early on, small but sufficient to showcase her talent and attributes. She quickly carved out a niche in parts that often required more preening for the camera than acting talent, but the films were respectable and popular.

And she'd grown comfortable. The roles she earned didn't invade her secret places, didn't require giving more of her heart than she had to give. She'd even turned down meatier roles, veering away from the turmoil of turning herself inside out emotionally for a film.

There was a certain safety in detachment, and Felicia clung to it. But all the money, success, fame, and attention of the last eight years hadn't erased the pain she'd felt growing up. She'd never stopped feeling like she had to prove herself. And she'd never found that sense of belonging that she was sure must be out there somewhere.

Felicia stepped dripping from the shower and toweled dry quickly. She grabbed up the comb on the counter and pulled it through her long, thick blond waves. The California sun had bleached her hair several shades lighter than it had been when she was growing up. Her skin was lightly tanned, her body flawlessly toned. On the outside, at least, she was nothing like the insecure, unfashionable girl who had run from Granbury eight years ago looking for recognition, and for validation of her self-worth.

She peered close into the mirror. At twenty-six, she still gloried in the prime of her golden good looks.

But maybe another couple of years and it would be time to start thinking about having her eyes done, or so the director on her last film had harshly pointed out to Felicia. She knew women who'd had it done already by their mid-twenties. Women who were afraid of losing their careers.

Women like Felicia.

Don't worry, she chided herself. *Worry doesn't help your looks.* She repeated automatically the words-to-live-by of her hard-bitten agent, Noreen. She was the only person Felicia had been able to count on since her grandmother had died. But Felicia wasn't naive enough to think Noreen would stick around if Felicia's career took a permanent nosedive. Noreen was too pragmatic for that.

The only true constant left in Felicia's life was Robin.

Felicia pulled on her silky soft underwear and then wrapped the dark blue terry-cloth robe around herself. Her pale hair spilled in lightly curling tendrils down her back.

She opened the bathroom door and listened down the hall. Light filtered in the wide back windows from the rising sun, casting a golden glow over the house. Silence met her ears.

Maybe Brandon had left.

Just the thought of him again sent an anxious trickle up her spine, along with a niggling sensation she pinpointed as guilt. Guilt and shame for the way she'd left him. She blocked the feelings off, as she had every time she'd thought of Brandon over the last eight years.

He would have eventually left her without a backward glance, she told herself. It was ridiculous to feel bad about leaving him.

She walked back out to the den and turned to creep softly up the stairs. It was amazing the commotion hadn't woken up Robin or Libby, she thought.

Poking her head into one of the two narrow, sloped-ceiling upstairs bedrooms, her eyes fell on the small sleeping form of her daughter. As she watched the gentle rise and fall of her five-year-old's breathing, she was suddenly struck by the immensity of what had just occurred out in the lake. If she had drowned, there would have been no one to care for Robin. No family. Nobody.

Robin needed her. No more flights of fancy or wild notions like taking off in a canoe alone at dawn without a life jacket. She didn't want Robin growing up searching for security like she had. She wanted Robin to know she belonged.

Felicia softly shut the door. No sound emanated from Libby's room either. Libby Hamilton had been Robin's nanny since she'd been born, and the young woman was highly dependable. One thing she wasn't known for, however, was sleeping light. She slept the sleep of the dead, Felicia often told her.

Turning back down the stairs, she wandered into the kitchen. Brandon leaned casually against the yellow counter, sipping coffee and staring out the window at the lake.

Felicia stopped short, surprised to see him still there. She'd convinced herself he'd left. The flutter in her stomach came alive again.

"I thought you'd be gone," she said, trying to keep her tone light.

"I told you I'd make coffee," he said. He stared at her enigmatically over his cup. She could feel his gaze, warm as the summer sun, raking over her robed form. He took another swallow and set the mug down. "Let me pour you a cup."

"I can get it myself," she said, moving to the pot of hot water on the stove.

Brandon reached around her, his arm brushing against her own with an electric shock. He picked up the spoon and measured out a teaspoon of instant coffee granules into her mug while Felicia poured the water over it.

She backed away, holding the mug tentatively to her lips. Checking the temperature, she took a grateful sip.

"Look, Brandon, thanks again for helping me out there," she began nervously. The cozy intimacy of morning coffee in the kitchen left her feeling uncomfortable and awkward.

Why wouldn't he leave?

"Just lucky I saw you," he answered. "I was out on the porch with my coffee, and I thought I saw something moving around out in the water. It was still pretty foggy, but then I heard you splashing." He frowned. "What were you doing out there? You know better than to get out in a lake by yourself with no life jacket."

His accusatory tone nettled Felicia.

"I was fine," she returned defensively. "I've always gone canoeing by myself, you know that. I just lost hold of the paddle, that's all."

Silence fell on the room.

"I'm—"

"Why did you—"

They both spoke at once, then silence.

"You go ahead," Felicia said.

Brandon took another sip of his coffee.

"All right," he said, placing his mug carefully on the counter. He looked at her seriously. "Why did you come back, Felicia?"

She met his eyes, then glanced down. She chewed her top lip.

"I don't know," she answered finally. She could tell him that she'd come back to show everyone in the town what a success she'd become. But she knew it was more than that.

She was still searching.

"You know about the Opera House benefit show, don't you?" Felicia asked.

"Everyone knows about that," Brandon said. He laughed shortly. "I haven't been back in town long myself, but I can tell you that the reopening of the Opera House, with you starring in the benefit show, is the talk of the town. It's been all over the local paper."

One corner of Felicia's mouth turned up ruefully.

"Yeah, papers love me," she said, half under her breath.

The flicker of knowledge in Brandon's blue eyes told her that he knew what she was referring to. For several years, the tabloid newspapers had been sporadically running stories, true and untrue, about her crumbling marriage, separation, and divorce from film star Rodney Kent. Rodney's star had slid while Felicia's had risen, and the divorce settlement Felicia had given her ex-husband had provided fodder for headlines across the country.

What had hurt the most wasn't that Rodney didn't love her. Down deep, Felicia knew she didn't love Rodney, either. The fact that he couldn't touch her deepest emotions had been part of his appeal, coupled with the dynamic screen magic they'd created together. It had seemed natural to transfer their partnership to real life.

What hurt was that he'd used her, taken advantage of her popularity for his own gain. In the end, he'd just wanted money.

"It's not all true, you know," she said, defensive again. "The stuff in the tabloids, I mean."

Brandon raised a brow.

"I wouldn't know," he said with a blasé shrug. "I don't buy them."

But he'd obviously seen the headlines that blared out at every grocery-store checkout stand, Felicia thought. Everyone had.

"What about you?" she asked, eager to change the subject. The last thing she wanted to do was explain to Brandon that she had been the miserable failure at marriage that she'd always known she'd be.

Or that money didn't buy happiness. Or a sense of belonging.

Suddenly, an idea ripped through her. Was Brandon here because—

"Did they ask you here to be in the show?" Felicia demanded.

Brandon's steady gaze met hers.

"The board didn't ask me here to star in the show with you, no," he answered. "Disappointed? Or relieved?" He watched her carefully.

Felicia shook her head, relaxing at his answer.

"Neither, of course," she told him, unwilling to share the reality of her relief with Brandon. "Why would I care?"

"You tell me," he said.

"I wouldn't have had a problem with you being in the show," Felicia said. "We've worked together before." She stopped, her breath catching strangely in her throat. She swallowed hard. "Everything that happened before, that's all in the past. Right?"

A barely perceptible hardening gleamed in Brandon's eyes. "Right. You put it all in the past pretty quick, didn't you, Felicia?" He sighed. "You married Rodney

Kent only about a year or so later." He shook his head. "Until then, I'd thought we had something special. I even thought you might come back. Crazy, huh?"

His tone was bitter. Not for the first time, Felicia felt overwhelmed with the knowledge that she'd hurt Brandon.

"I'm sorry—"

"Forget it," he said, brushing away her offer of apology as if it were of no importance to him. "I don't need it. It wouldn't have worked out anyway. Young love, you know. Or whatever it was. It wasn't love, obviously."

Felicia stiffened.

"Right," she said.

Silence reared up again.

"Mommy? Who's that man?"

Felicia turned to the small voice.

"Robin." Felicia knelt down and hugged the little girl. Her curly blond locks tumbled around her chubby face in tangled disarray. Hazel eyes, round and questioning, were staring at Brandon.

"This is Brandon Donnelly," Felicia said quickly. "He's our neighbor. He just stopped by to say hello."

Brandon smiled at Robin, and she smiled back easily. He bent over and held his hand out to the little girl.

"How do you do?" he asked, shaking her hand.

She smiled up at Felicia.

"I like him," Robin announced.

"This is my daughter, Robin," Felicia said, meeting Brandon's eyes defiantly.

"I thought I heard you up," Libby's voice came from around the corner as she headed into the kitchen. The young redhead stopped short at the sight of Brandon.

Felicia introduced the two, noticing the sparkle in

Libby's eyes as she shook hands with Brandon. For some reason, it irritated her to see Libby's appreciation of his looks.

She'd never minded how excited Libby got about meeting the celebrities that occasionally stopped by her L.A. home. But she found herself unusually annoyed by Libby's reaction to Brandon.

"Brandon was just leaving," Felicia said, frustrated with herself as much as with Libby. She turned to Brandon. "Thank you again. Maybe I'll see you some other time before I leave. I'll only be in town a short while, until the show is over."

Brandon nodded coolly, as if seeing her again was a matter of little consequence to his life.

"I'll take care of the canoe," he said.

Felicia had completely forgotten about the canoe she'd left floating in the cove. She told him not to worry about it, but he ignored her. With a generous smile to Libby and Robin, he left, letting the back door bang shut behind him.

Felicia breathed a sigh of relief and gratitude at his departure. Trailing into the den, she shoved aside the dustcover from the couch and plopped down onto it, staring at the closed back door.

Thank goodness he's gone, she thought. If she was lucky, she could avoid him the rest of her stay. After all, she wouldn't be home much. She'd be far too busy at the Opera House, rehearsing for the show, to hang around at home. In fact, she'd make a point of not hanging around the house.

She glanced down at the floor, noticing the puddle where he'd stood in his underwear, water dripping down his long muscular thighs and calves. Squeezing her eyes tight to block out the relentless image, she realized the hopelessness of her effort.

Brandon Donnelly was in town. There was no ignoring him.

Brandon inhaled the crisp morning air as he stepped down from Felicia's back porch, struggling to free his body and mind from the temptation of Felicia's freshly showered scent. He stopped a moment, staring out at the pristine stillness of Lake Granbury.

He remembered how she'd felt in his arms as he carried her from the shore, soft and small against his chest. Confused feelings rioted within him. One part of him was angry with her, even after all this time. Yet a secret, hidden part of him had yearned for this moment for eight years, the moment when he would hold Felicia in his arms again.

And he'd almost told her the truth of why he was in Granbury. If she'd just seemed happy to see him, or even mildly content, he would have told her.

But she hadn't been happy to see him. That much was abundantly clear. And so Brandon had held back. She'd find out soon enough why he was in town.

Brandon inhaled another deep, fresh breath.

Yes, she'd find out soon enough.

TWO

"Who was that totally gorgeous hunk?" Libby cooed as she breezed into the den. She crossed the room quickly and peered out the window to watch Brandon. Following Libby's gaze, Felicia turned and saw him rowing out in a small boat to retrieve the wayward canoe.

"He's just a neighbor, like I said," Felicia answered slowly, narrowing her eyes as she watched Brandon row his small craft through the water with quick, powerful strokes.

"He's not 'just' anything," Libby said, turning from the window and sitting down beside Felicia. "I can't believe your luck, Felicia. To have a neighbor like that! You've always got the greatest men." Libby put her hand to her mouth quickly, reddening. "I mean, except for Rodney, of course."

Libby thought every time a co-star of Felicia's dropped by to see her that it meant Felicia was dating him. She never seemed to quite believe Felicia when she tried to convince her that her life wasn't as exciting as Libby would like to think it was.

Felicia shook her head.

"He's not mine," Felicia said. "At least, not anymore."

She instantly regretted the slip.

"What do you mean, 'anymore'? Did you know him before when you lived here? You did, didn't you? Did you two have a thing? Did you have an affair with him?" Libby shot the questions out in a quick staccato of words.

Felicia sighed and stood.

"I didn't mean that," she said. "I knew him. We dated a few times. That was it. It was nothing." She hoped she'd minimized the situation sufficiently for Libby. "We were just friends, really."

Friends who had been lovers, Felicia finished silently. Friends who had contemplated marriage. Now they couldn't even be friends.

"So I can have him?" Libby asked eagerly.

Felicia laughed harshly.

"Have him?" she repeated. Felicia stared at the twenty-three-year-old. She stemmed the rising swell of possessiveness she felt. What did she care if Robin's nanny was interested in Brandon Donnelly? If Brandon wanted her, Libby could have him. "He's not mine to give, Libby," she said sternly. "But if you're asking if I care, then the answer is no." A sharp jab of pain twisted through her stomach. She couldn't resist adding, "We're not going to be here that long, you know, Libby. There's hardly time for a deep and meaningful relationship."

"There's enough time for me," Libby said, a pleased smile spreading her lips.

Felicia forced a careless shrug and rose, moving back to her bedroom. Glancing out the window of her room, she saw Brandon heading back toward the shore, towing her canoe behind his rowboat.

She looked away.

So much for coming home, she thought. If she had to run into Brandon Donnelly, maybe it was best it was in the beginning, after all. She wouldn't have to worry about a chance encounter with him now. It was over. Finished.

She'd wondered about him for years. Now she could close the chapter for good.

Moving slowly, she carefully hung up the dresses and blouses she'd brought with her. She selected a soft cotton sundress for her appearance at the Opera House office. Sliding the cool flower-patterned dress over her head, her thoughts again drifted to her next-door neighbor.

It wouldn't have worked out anyway. . . . It wasn't love.

Had he meant those words?

How many times had she wondered how her life would have been different if she'd stayed in Granbury and married Brandon? She couldn't have become a successful film star. And maybe he wouldn't have gained respect in musical theater. Or perhaps he would have expected her to give up her Hollywood dream and follow him to New York. After all, he'd asked her to stay in Granbury for him.

Back then, he'd said he wanted the slow, country life. He'd wanted Felicia, a passel of kids, and regional theater. His idealized plans hadn't provided much room for Felicia's dreams. He hadn't understood her need for Hollywood, for fame and success.

She had to prove she was someone. Brandon had never understood that deep-seated thirst for recognition. Even in his New York career, Felicia had noticed he'd chosen roles he wanted, character roles with depth, shying away from parts that could have provided more popular exposure. Yet he'd received a large measure of recognition anyway, through his quiet dedication and unwavering talent.

Felicia also knew that Brandon couldn't understand her need to find a place where she could belong. He'd been born in Granbury, raised by two loving parents. He fit in.

She wondered again why he'd left Granbury. Surely not because she had left.

She snorted indelicately.

Right.

With meticulous care, she applied her makeup with the skill learned from experts in the business. The manicured, stylish woman she had become in the last eight years was reflected back at her in the mirror. No one was going to confuse this Felicia with the one they'd known eight years ago.

She dropped a quick peck on Robin's rosy cheek and waved at Libby as she passed. Outside, the morning air was still crisp but starting to hint at the warmth to come. In a few hours, Felicia expected, the summer day would be in full swing. Two cars rested side by side in the driveway. She'd rented a silver Mercedes for herself and a bright red Blazer for Libby to use to run around with Robin.

After settling into the rented Mercedes, Felicia backed the vehicle out, noticing there wasn't a car in front of Brandon's house. She hadn't seen one there when they'd pulled in last night, either, so she figured he kept his car in the garage.

Felicia drove slowly, soaking in the sights on her way into town. Last night, when they had driven in from the airport, it had been too dark to see anything of the landscape, and their route had taken them only to the outskirts of Granbury. As Felicia guided the car downtown, her eyes picked up first on the many things that had changed. The old iron bridge was gone, replaced by a new, wide concrete overpass. New businesses and homes dotted the landscape, crowding the lakeshore. The signs of increased population struck her everywhere.

But as she approached the town square on Main Street, she began to see more-familiar landmarks. The old burger joint by the lake where you could pull up in your boat and hop out for a quick hot lunch, the waterfront hotels, the beautiful turn-of-the-century Victorian homes. Memories rushed over her all at once.

Shopping downtown with her grandmother, picnics and July Fourth parades around the courthouse, even a hazy memory of a treat at the ice cream parlor on the square with her mother. She could never remember what her mother had said that final day. But she remembered the ice cream. The rich sugar cone. Fudge chocolate nut. Two scoops. The unexpected goodbye afterward.

And then there were other memories. Moonlit car rides with Brandon over the softly rolling hills, lovemaking under the brilliant Georgia stars . . . but never a goodbye.

A few minutes later, Felicia pulled up at the town square, which was dominated by the century-old limestone courthouse. Parking in the lot that wrapped around the building, she stood up out of the car and took a deep breath.

The restored town square bustled with summer tourists and local shoppers strolling down the sidewalks and gazing into the windows of the small antique and specialty stores. The Opera House stood tall and elegant amid the shops, as it had for over a hundred years.

Felicia walked across the square, the wind blowing softly through her long hair and twisting her dress between her legs. She pulled the Opera House door open boldly, holding her head high and proud. Several tourists idled in the foyer, heads bent over historical pamphlets. They looked up, eyes widening as they recognized Felicia. She cheerily bestowed a broad, gracious smile at the onlookers and headed toward the young woman at the ticket window.

"Felicia!"

Felicia turned, seeing a tall, silver-haired woman hurrying toward her across the narrow lobby.

"Lola Dunbar, president of the Opera board. You remember me, don't you, dear? I wrote you and spoke to you on the telephone several times," the woman said, grasping Felicia's hand warmly in her own. "I'm so glad to see you made it all right. How was your trip?"

Felicia smiled and assured her that her trip had been lovely. She remembered Lola Dunbar. Or she remembered Lola Dunbar's daughter, anyway. A high school cheerleader. Pretty, popular, and blessed with doting parents, Dory Dunbar had always seemed to have it all.

"I'm so glad to be here," Felicia said.

"And we're so lucky to have you," Lola gushed. "Come right this way. Our director's expecting you. Well, he's our temporary director for now, but we're so hoping that we can convince him to stay on as our permanent managing director. He simply insisted we get you to come for the benefit show, and we all agreed."

She slipped her arm through Felicia's as they walked around to the office. In a lowered voice, she continued,

"Everyone on the Opera board is so delighted to have both of you back. The name recognition that both of you have, coupled with your roots in Granbury, will help us bring in old and new backers for the Opera House. We're so optimistic that with your help we're going to get the Opera House back on its feet."

Felicia crinkled her brow. What did Lola mean— "both" of them?

Lola guided her into a small, low-ceilinged room stuffed with boxes of programs, books, and posters. A tall man stood with his back turned, talking on the phone as they entered.

Felicia stared at the man, her heart beginning a wild beat. She longed to turn and run but felt rooted to the spot.

Brandon pivoted to face Felicia, hanging up the phone. He'd been waiting for her. His mind hadn't been free of her since the moment he'd pulled her from the water of Lake Granbury.

Nor had he wanted his mind to be free of her. In an instant, she'd reclaimed an unyielding hold on his senses.

"Hello, Felicia." Brandon met the surprise in her misty green eyes, then his gaze swept down over the soft curves that rose above the flowered dress and back up to her face.

His memory of the morning hadn't been wrong. She was more beautiful now than she'd been eight years ago. In films, she'd appeared glorious, like a goddess. He'd told himself it wasn't real, that it was make-believe, the tricks of makeup and lighting. Felicia had been a pretty, fresh-faced young girl. Not gorgeous. Just a pretty country girl.

But now he'd seen Felicia face-to-face. Here, in reality, she'd seemed like Venus at dawn as he'd rescued her from the lake. Gone was the simple country girl. In front of him was the goddess.

What hadn't changed was the haunting, lost quality in her eyes. He remembered that look in her eyes from eight years ago. It was still there.

"Brandon?" The name escaped Felicia's lips as a breathy question.

She sounded bewildered. She looked scared. Her frozen stance reminded him of the way he'd seen rabbits freeze when he walked out into the yard suddenly at dusk. Freeze, then run when he tried to come closer.

Brandon stretched out a hand to indicate a faded orange, slightly torn cushioned chair in front of his desk.

"Please, sit down," he invited Felicia.

"She just arrived," Lola put in from where she stood near the doorway. "I found her in the lobby. I told her already all about how glad we are to have her with us, but I know you'll want to tell her, too. I was just telling Felicia about how you particularly wanted her to come, and how you were the one who came up with her name when we started looking for a celebrity to headline the first show."

Brandon nodded, his blue eyes intently focused on Felicia's face. She looked ready to run.

"Absolutely," he murmured. "I wouldn't have considered anyone else."

Brandon once again waved toward the lumpy orange chair across from his desk. Felicia licked her lips, the movement of her tongue a nervous rose shimmer over her mouth. She swallowed and sat down.

"Well, I'll leave you two alone to discuss the show," Lola said. "I'm meeting some of the Opera board members over at The Tea Room across the square. They'll be so pleased to know Felicia is here. Perhaps you'll have a chance to stop over there and meet some of our members in a little while. If not, I know they'll all look forward to seeing you at the fundraiser—the Opera House Ball—tomorrow night, Felicia."

With a wave of her heavily jeweled hand, Lola was off.

"You're the director?" Felicia asked, a confused frown marring her brow.

Her halting voice revealed her shock at his presence in the Opera House. A sense of guilt niggled at Brandon. He should have told her earlier, so she would have been prepared.

"Yes." Brandon forced a smile. "Of course."

He could see the confusion still clouding her eyes. After what he'd told her earlier, he knew she hadn't been expecting to see him here.

But he'd known she'd be here. He'd wanted her here. When he'd been asked to help revitalize the Opera House by coming on board as the temporary director, his first thought had been to bring Felicia in for the benefit show.

She'd tiptoed through his thoughts for years. Sometimes he'd recalled her with anger, especially in the beginning, but often he'd remembered her with regret. After she'd left him, he'd left Granbury as well, disillusioned and unhappy.

In New York, he'd had more than his fair measure of success. But recognition and money hadn't eased the void left by Felicia. He'd tried to fill it with other women, but he'd never found anyone who could fill it up so far that Felicia's memory hadn't found room to sneak back in.

Coming home to help the local theater was just the change he had needed. He was already thinking of staying on permanently. It felt good to be home. This was where he had started, where he belonged. He'd come full circle.

And he'd wanted to see Felicia again. Maybe seeing her again was the only way he'd ever wipe her from his subconscious fantasies. But he'd been afraid that if she knew he was involved, she wouldn't come. So he'd let the Opera board handle all contact with Felicia. She didn't know he was directing the benefit show.

He had the advantage. He'd wanted it that way. And now Felicia was obviously struggling to deal with the surprise.

She shook her head as she stared across the desk at Brandon, as if shaking off cobwebs. She couldn't believe her eyes. Brandon? He'd lied to her!

"You told me you weren't involved in the show," she accused. "What's going on here?"

"Well," Brandon said slowly, rubbing his chin with one hand as if thinking ponderously as he spoke. "What we're doing here is putting on a benefit show for the Opera House, which is in serious financial trouble—"

"I know that!" Felicia's voice came out high and frustrated. She took a deep breath. "Brandon, what is this all about? You're the director? You said—"

"I said the Opera board didn't ask me to come to Granbury to star in the benefit with you." Brandon shot out a brief smile. "And that's the truth. I do plan on performing in the show, but that's not the primary reason I'm here. The Opera board asked me here to take on the management and direction, temporarily, of the Opera House. It was later when I decided to bring you out to perform in the show."

Nervous trembles clenched at Felicia's stomach. He'd admitted it. He was the one who'd brought her back to Granbury.

She never would have come if she'd known, she thought. Her mouth felt dry as denials tumbled about her mind. *Maybe she would have come. Maybe she'd wanted to see him.*

"You were behind asking me to come back to Granbury?"

"Why should that surprise you?" he asked. His blue eyes held hers for what seemed like a long moment.

"Why me?" Felicia asked, returning his question with a question. Her heart was beginning to pound again, so loud she wondered if Brandon could hear it, or if he could see it through her low-cut sundress.

"I know better than anyone what a wonderful actress you are," Brandon said, a bitter edge to his words. "I've had the first-hand treatment, haven't I?"

Felicia stared back at him speechlessly.

"But we're wasting time, aren't we?" he continued. "Let's get to the benefit show."

His abrupt switch to business left Felicia floored. She was still groping to understand that Brandon was the director of the Opera House. The bare bulb in the low ceiling cast an almost blinding white light over the small room, making Felicia's eyes ache.

Or was it her head that was aching? she wondered. Or maybe her heart.

"Wait," she said. "You didn't say anything about this when I saw you earlier. Why didn't you tell me you were the director of the Opera House?"

Brandon shrugged.

"You didn't ask," he said simply. "And you know now."

"But—" she began, still not satisfied.

"We'll be doing a three-week run of *Passion's Pride*," Brandon said over her voice, naming a popular recent Broadway play. He reached down into a large cardboard box and pulled out a script. He slapped the thick script down onto the desk in front of Felicia.

She picked up the play. His skirting of her questions frustrated her, but the mention of *Passion's Pride* jolted her into attention.

Passion's Pride was the tale of a dramatic love triangle. The play opens with a career-oriented reporter, Veronica, returning from a stint in a war zone with hopes of reigniting the flame with her former lover, Stefan. Coming close to death overseas has finally turned Veronica's thoughts to settling down with Stefan, but she finds that Stefan is already involved with another woman, Angel. The play follows the struggle as Stefan is forced to choose between the two women, ending with his decision to remain with the charmingly seductive Angel.

Reports had circulated that Felicia's name had come up for consideration for the role of the sweetly appealing Angel in the forthcoming film version. The prospect of Felicia playing Angel in the Opera House production had been the only facet of the deal that had appeased her agent, Noreen, when Felicia had insisted on taking part in the benefit show. Noreen knew exactly how to use a charity run as Angel to help Felicia land the plum film role.

Winning the movie part would be just the boost Felicia's career needed. After four smash hits in a row, her last two movies had been dangerously slow at the box office. The film adaptation of *Passion's Pride* was destined to be a success.

Brandon sat back in his chair and propped his long legs against the top of his desk. "You'll be playing Veronica, of course," he said.

Felicia's eyes popped wide. Veronica? The outwardly

tough, inwardly emotion-torn character that loses everything in the end? *Veronica?*

She didn't play characters like Veronica. She played Angel roles, parts requiring simplicity, humor, charm, good looks.

"No," she said firmly, the refusal emerging from some visceral, protective place within her. "I have to play Angel."

Brandon raised one dark brow quirkily. He ran a leisurely hand through his thick, wavy brown hair, then lightly tapped a pencil against his lips. The ferocity of her response unnerved him momentarily, but he was determined not to reveal his reaction to her.

He wanted Felicia to play Veronica. His theatrical instincts told him the part was right for her. He'd seen every film she'd made, and he knew from his experience with her at the Opera House years ago that she possessed depths she'd never tapped on film. She always held something back in her movies, and he was determined to see her perform at the Opera House again with the dramatic power that he knew she held.

He'd only seen hints of that power in her performances in those days, but he knew she had it. And somehow she'd lost it, or hidden it away. He wanted to see in Felicia the woman he'd once known. Maybe then he could put her in the past once and for all and leave her haunting eyes behind him.

"You'll play Veronica," he repeated. "The show's already been cast."

Felicia stood up, not even realizing she'd done so until she found herself looking down at Brandon. He continued leaning back, his legs propped, gazing at her with an obnoxiously smug expression.

He rested the pencil on the desk in a gesture of finality.

Felicia shook her head, the movement unconscious. "I'm Angel," she said. "I can't play Veronica."

"Why not?" Brandon asked, his countenance unfathomably blank.

"Why not?" Felicia repeated. Why not? Was he crazy? "What are you thinking? What did you get me here for? How can you have someone else play Angel?"

"You're an actress, aren't you?" he demanded. "You can play any part. You can play Stefan if I ask you to."

"And I'd rather play Stefan than play Veronica," Felicia returned heatedly.

"Well, I'm sorry to tell you that you can't. That role's been cast already as well," Brandon told her. "I'm playing Stefan."

"You!"

"Yes, me," Brandon replied calmly.

Was that a smirk on his face? Felicia seethed inside. She mentally scoured through the play, recalling the intimate scenes played out between Stefan and his ex-lover, Veronica.

Scenes Brandon planned to play out with Felicia. In public.

In public. Felicia's eyes narrowed.

"You know that Veronica is out of character for me," Felicia said coolly. "And she's certainly not the best part. Who's playing Angel?"

"Just one of the regular company players," Brandon said. "I've managed to bring back most of the old company. Some of them had already scattered to other theaters, but she's one of the old regulars. She's not a star of your caliber, don't worry. You won't be outshone."

His sarcasm rang harshly in her ears.

"You're upstaging me with an unknown?" she asked quickly.

"Ego, ego," Brandon murmured. Angry, Felicia was even more beautiful, he thought. He watched as she flipped back the wavy locks of unruly blond hair that fell about her shoulders, glowing like sweet honey in the bright office light. Her cheeks flushed rosily under the thin layer of carefully applied makeup.

Felicia glared down at him. Ego! Who was he to talk about ego, lounging casually at his desk as if she were just some bit player throwing a tantrum?

"My ego!" she sputtered out at last. "How dare you!"

Brandon chuckled softly. What a tigress she was, he thought. He didn't remember this side of her. She'd always been demure, quiet. One thing was clear—she'd learned to fight for herself in the last eight years.

"I really don't see why you're so upset," he said serenely. "You won't be upstaged. Don't worry."

Okay, hold on, Felicia, she warned herself as she felt an immense tide of frustration welling up inside her against the man in front of her. He's the director. She knew how to handle directors.

She smiled. It felt a little stretched on her lips, but she was sure it looked fine.

She sat.

And breathed deep.

"Brandon," she began, her voice like refined sugar. "Maybe you don't know, but there's a screen adaptation of *Passion's Pride* in the works right now as we speak. I'm up for the role of Angel. It would be a fabulous vehicle for me, as I'm sure you can imagine. Think of the press you could get for the benefit show if it got out that I was playing Angel here in Granbury at the Opera House."

Felicia smiled again, this time a real smile of anticipation at landing the film role of Angel.

"Gossip simply flies in this business, you know," she continued. "People would say I was preparing for the film role. It would do wonders for business at the Opera House."

Brandon picked up the pencil again and tapped it against his jean-clad knee. He appeared to consider Felicia's argument.

He put down the pencil, at the same time shifting his legs from his desktop to the floor. He straightened in his seat.

"You'll play Veronica," he announced.

Felicia expelled the breath she'd been holding. Anger surged up again.

"Why? Just tell me why?" she insisted. "I don't understand. You brought me here because I'm a celebrity, but you hand the best role to someone else. It doesn't make sense."

Brandon met her searching gaze. He remained unperturbed, as if her reaction didn't bother him in the least, as if he'd known she'd react this way, expected it.

Planned it.

He insisted we get you to come, Lola Dunbar had said.

"You're doing this to me on purpose," Felicia said slowly, grinding out each word. "You want to get even with me. You want to humiliate me."

"Not true," he responded. It couldn't be further from the truth. But he couldn't possibly explain to Felicia that his desire to challenge her cloaked his own need to free himself. Angel was typical of all the roles Felicia had played since leaving Granbury. Brandon had read reports of roles she'd turned down, and he knew she shied away from parts requiring high emotional intensity.

The way she'd managed her career reminded him of the painfully shy, sensitive girl he'd known long ago. He'd always suspected that there was something deep in her heart that had hurt her, and still hurt her. The lost look in her eyes had never left.

He'd wondered sometimes if the answer to why she'd left him so abruptly eight years ago lay in the hidden hurt in her eyes. They'd grown so close that summer, closer than he'd ever been to any woman before or since. He'd asked her to marry him, and she'd disappeared from his life. He still wondered why.

"Then why are you doing this?" Felicia demanded, arms crossed tightly over her chest. "Why would you engineer my coming here? No one mentioned you were the director. Lola made all the arrangements, never mentioning your name. Now that I'm here, supposedly to raise money for the Opera House, you throw me into a role I don't want. How can you be so petty, Brandon?"

He shook his head.

"Is it Hollywood that has made you so paranoid, Felicia?" he asked. "Angel isn't right for you. Veronica is. It's not a lesser role. Veronica is the best part for you. That's all there is to it."

"What are you talking about?"

"Veronica has more depth," he said. "It's the most demanding role. My other players couldn't handle the part."

Felicia barely heard the words over the rush of anger she felt.

"Eight years, Brandon. I'm sorry. Okay?" She sighed. "And, by the way, Veronica is pathetic."

"No," Brandon said, ignoring the apology. "Veronica is a mature character who learns to face the consequences of her decisions.''

''She's a loser,'' Felicia said flatly. ''Don't you realize that this will cost me the film, Brandon? The producers of the screen version will find out that I'm playing Veronica, in a small-town production, no less. And upstaged by an unknown!''

She leaned across the desk.

''If you ever cared about me, Brandon, don't do this,'' she said. The words were pleading, but the tone of her voice was firm, cool. If there was one thing she'd learned in the entertainment industry, it was not to beg. Let them know you were down, and you'd end up in worse trouble than you started out in, Noreen always said.

''You'll play Veronica,'' he said again.

She stared at him with unbelieving eyes. The Brandon she had remembered all these years wouldn't have used her this way, to satisfy his own vengeance. But this Brandon would. This Brandon had waited eight years to find a way to hurt her.

''I can't believe what you've become,'' she said. ''Vengeful. Spiteful.''

''I'm not interested in revenge. Veronica is the right part for you,'' he repeated. He laughed again, a low, strangely unhappy sound. ''Your imagination is working overtime, Felicia. That was eight years ago, as you pointed out. Are you so egotistical that you actually think I've waited all these years to find a way to avenge myself?''

Felicia froze.

''I can't believe this,'' she said. ''I'm not playing Veronica, Brandon. You're not ruining my career.''

She stood up again.

''I'm out of this, Brandon. Give the Opera board my

regrets.'' She turned toward the door. If she had to look at his handsome, smirking face another minute, she wouldn't be responsible for her actions. To think that she'd been tempted to go all soft and gooey remembering their past together!

''I don't think so,'' Brandon said, unflappable as ever. ''Not unless you want it splashed all over the papers that you walked out on a benefit show for the cultural heartbeat of your old hometown.''

Felicia turned around slowly.

''You made a commitment to the Opera House, Felicia, remember?'' A note of warning entered Brandon's tone. His indigo eyes gleamed darkly. ''How would it look if you reneged on the arrangement, left your hometown high and dry when they needed you? Especially when you have a film deal pending. A film you need.''

His challenge hung in the air between them, like a sword pointed at Felicia's throat.

THREE

The expression of horror on Felicia's face at his threat to go public if she walked out on the benefit show knifed at Brandon's gut, but he couldn't back down. If she left now, he'd never know what had happened eight years ago. And he'd never be free of her memory.

"The papers could make a lot of a star walking off a charity show for her hometown," he forced himself to say softly.

"You wouldn't do it." But a good look at the straight line of his mouth and the chiseled hardness of his jaw sent a nervous dread slicing through her chest.

"Are you sure about that?" Brandon asked coolly.

He'd do it, Felicia thought numbly.

Why hadn't she asked who was the new Opera House director? She hadn't even given it a thought. She'd expected, of course, to be handed a peachy role as the star. She hadn't thought she'd be tricked into the role of Veronica. She hadn't known Brandon would be the director.

Or that the last eight years would have filled him with so much spite for her.

Felicia met Brandon's firm stare. His vivid blue eyes held a strange, penetrating sharpness. Hard, she thought.

Where was the softness with which he'd once gazed down at her during all those long, hot summer evenings spent beside the lake? How he must detest her now, to try to ruin her this way.

"I'll go to the Opera board," Felicia said. "What's best for me is also what's best for the Opera House."

"Go ahead," Brandon said, shrugging. "I have total autonomy in casting and direction. See if Lola cares when you tell her you want the part of Angel. I can assure you she's not likely to look on this little brouhaha favorably, considering her daughter Dory is playing Angel."

"Dory?"

This is a nightmare, she thought. Dory Dunbar!

"You're not serious," Felicia muttered, hardly able to believe her ears.

Dory Dunbar. Lola Dunbar's cheerleading daughter. Dory, the same age as Felicia, had been the star of every single high school play. She'd also been the president of the drama club. Felicia thought—no, knew—she was a better performer than Dory. But in those days it hadn't mattered.

Dory was the daughter of Frank and Lola Dunbar, wealthy and established citizens who also happened to have their fingertips on the pulse of the local arts community with their ties to the Opera House. It seemed a natural progression for Dory to reign centerstage in school productions.

An old, familiar, knotted-up feeling encircled Felicia's heart. Recognizing the feeling for what it was—envy—didn't improve her mood. It had been a long time since the days when Felicia had felt inferior to pretty, popular Dory. Now it was as if the years had simply fallen away and she was the same insecure girl she'd been when she was growing up in Granbury.

"I'm absolutely serious," Brandon was saying. "Why not?"

"Dory's playing Angel?"

"I understand she's a perfectly fine performer. She was part of the Opera House company for a number of years after we'd both left." He cast Felicia a pointed gaze. "She's been out of theater for about a year, but I think—"

"But you could have me play Angel!" Felicia cried, still unable to give up on the part. "I'm more experienced."

"That's why you're playing Veronica," Brandon returned.

Several moments of dead silence followed this final repetition of his intent for Felicia to play Veronica. How could she possibly get out of this? Felicia wondered. What would Noreen say if she left and the press got a whiff of the news? Noreen would be furious.

Noreen had been none too pleased in the first place with Felicia's announcement that she was returning to her hometown to take part in a community-theater production. But Felicia had been determined. Her long fight with Rodney to settle the divorce had drained her, followed by two mediocre films. She'd wanted out, away from the frenetic pace of her life in L.A., away from the negative press and the pressure, just for a little while.

And she'd wanted to return to her hometown and show everyone how successful she'd become. Perhaps here, in Granbury, she could figure out why all her success hadn't made her happy.

That is, if she could still consider herself a success after the last two pictures. A part of her feared that her career had peaked, that she was on the downward slide.

But her return to Granbury, instead of instilling new vigor into her career, seemed doomed to sound the death knell. Playing Veronica would be lethal. The only thing worse might be not playing Veronica. Leaving and breaking an agreement for a charity benefit in her hometown would be nothing but fodder for the tabloids. That kind of press would be ruinous, not only for her prospects of getting the film role of Angel, but for her chances at any future role.

She doubted she'd get Angel now, after being cast as Veronica in a community-theater production. *What fun the papers will have with that!* she thought bitterly.

There was absolutely no way to win here. And she had to consider other roles after Angel.

Felicia looked again at Brandon. He was sitting at his desk, idly examining a copy of the play as if she wasn't even in the room.

The silence of the last few moments roared in Brandon's ears as he studied the script with unseeing eyes. He felt the air crackle between them. He smelled her soft, floral scent. It took all the strength within him not to lift his eyes to her, to wait as if he didn't care what her response would be.

If she said no, he'd have to let her go. He would never hurt her through the press. She'd had too much of that. He could hardly believe she would even give credit to his threat.

And if she didn't, she'd disappear from his life again as she had eight years before. That prospect loomed up dark and heavy inside his heart.

"All right," he heard her say at last. She slid into the chair across from his desk. "I'll play Veronica.

But only because I have no choice. Because you're blackmailing me."

Brandon raised his gaze to Felicia, his heart lifting as if a cement block had been removed from his chest.

"I'd hardly call holding you to your word blackmailing you," he said, hiding his relief. He stood. "Now, since we have this all settled, why don't we mosey across the square to The Tea Room and try to catch some of the Opera board members? It would be a good opportunity for you to meet a few of them before the ball on Saturday night. They're eager to see you, I'm sure."

Felicia picked up her copy of the play and stood again. She felt Brandon's eyes move up and down her form in a methodical, calculating manner. Just as Felicia began to grow annoyed and was opening her mouth to tell him so, he nodded.

"I thought so," he murmured. "You do look a bit slimmer than I remembered. And a little blonder." He stared at her hair. "But I suppose Hollywood is the land of illusion."

"I don't dye my hair!" Felicia retorted hotly. "What makes you think you can—"

"And I'd have to say you do look different in other areas as well," he added, his gaze settling obviously on her chest, following the curve and dip of skin along the low-scooped neckline of her sundress. He shifted his eyes back up to meet her shocked expression. He grinned.

Felicia tried to speak but could only sputter angrily for a moment. She finally managed to get out a few disjointed words. "I certainly have not! I never! How dare you!"

"Just checking," he said, chuckling. "Nothing to get all hot and bothered about."

Brandon's heart lurched as he observed Felicia's fiery expression. He'd only been half teasing in his remarks. If her beauty had been artificial, perhaps the traitorous response she provoked in the pit of his stomach would quiet.

He came around the side of the desk and walked toward the door of his office. Felicia was there before him, and as she stepped out into the hall, Brandon slipped his arm casually around her and guided her toward the outer door. She fit against him like smooth velvet. A rush of remembered sensations floated over him.

They'd worked at the Opera House together before, and she'd been his then. They'd spent stolen hours after the show making passionate, tender love in secret spots before he'd bring her home to her grandmother's house. Brandon had kept a thick, downy quilt in his pickup truck, and they'd found a hidden clearing alongside the lake where their only intrusions were the lapping of the water and the deep hooting of the night owls. And the soft sounds of love.

At least, he'd thought it was love. It had been love for him.

Felicia tried to shrug off Brandon's arm, but he wouldn't release her. Short of making a scene in front of passersby, she had to put up with what seemed to her to be his smugly obtuse gallantry. He seemed completely unaware of how irritated she was with him.

Brandon guided her down the sidewalk and across the street to another side of the square, weaving around tourists and shoppers as he chitchatted aimlessly about local politics. In front of a candlemaking shop, Felicia stopped short, incensed by his nonchalant insensitivity.

"What are you talking about?" she demanded. "I don't care. Why would I care about the city council, or the mayor, or anything else around here? I'm just here to play this benefit, and then I'm out of here. And it won't be a minute too soon, I'm sure."

Brandon stared down at her. The bright morning sun glinted in his dark hair, picking up light sun streaks along the sides near his face. Felicia was moved again by how handsome he was.

Don't think that, she warned herself. *Don't be sucked in. He wants to hurt you, and don't forget it.*

"I just thought you might be interested," Brandon was saying. "I've enjoyed catching up on local news since I've been back. It's your town, too."

"It stopped being my town a long time ago," Felicia replied. "And you can stop playing this little game of chatting with me. We don't have to play nice with each other when we're alone."

"I'm sorry you feel that way."

"Well, I do," she returned. "What do you expect? You know how I feel about playing Veronica. You know what you're doing to my career. On purpose. Just to hurt me."

Her accusation that he was trying to hurt her took his breath away like he'd been socked in the abdomen. Hurting her was the last thing he wanted. His grip on her arm tightened.

"Come on," he said gruffly, propelling her down the sidewalk. When they stood in front of the antique shop and tea room, Brandon reached out with his free hand and opened the tall door.

Cool air swept over Felicia's body as she entered The Tea Room. An eclectic mix of antiques, homespun country crafts, specialty gift items, and timeworn pieces of furniture filled the high-ceilinged shop. Several shoppers meandered at a leisurely pace, touching and looking as they made their way through the store.

The door creaked shut behind them, and Brandon nudged Felicia toward the rear of the shop. A grouping of quaint cloth-covered tables occupied the back half of the building. At their approach, Lola Dunbar waved as she rose from a long table. A half-dozen ladies turned their curious gazes toward Felicia and Brandon.

"Felicia! Brandon! I'm so glad you were able to stop by to see us. I've just been telling the ladies how lucky we are to have the two of you working with us to reopen the Opera House." Lola beamed as she spoke. In quick succession, she introduced Felicia to each of her friends. "There are many more members of the Opera board, of course," she said, her crimson-painted lips spread in a wide smile. "You'll meet more of them tomorrow."

"I'm so glad to see you," one silver-haired woman said in a high, trembly voice. She squeezed Felicia's hand warmly. "You may not remember me, dear, but I knew your grandmother."

"Agnes Parks," Felicia repeated the name slowly. "Oh, yes, I do remember you, Mrs. Parks. You were in Grandmother's garden club."

"That's right," Mrs. Parks agreed, clearly pleased that Felicia had placed her. "Your grandmother always grew the most lovely pink roses. Are her rosebushes still alive?"

Felicia thought back. She didn't remember noticing the rosebushes. But, then, she hadn't really had a chance to look around the yard yet.

"I'm really not sure," she told Mrs. Parks hesitantly.

"I still miss your grandmother," Mrs. Parks added.

Felicia felt a lump in her chest. It had been a long time since she'd been around anyone who knew what a wonderful person her grandmother had been. Her grandmother hadn't lived long enough in California to develop any friendships there before she died.

"I do, too," Felicia said softly.

Brandon, his hand still linked through her arm, pressed his fingers lightly against her. Felicia glanced up at him. His eyes on hers felt warm, sympathetic. He remembered her grandmother, too.

Felicia turned away, not wanting sympathy from Brandon.

"Sit down," Lola said, waving toward two empty chairs at the end of the table.

Brandon drew out a chair, waiting until Felicia sat before settling beside her. A bouncy young waitress came by and returned again quickly with a cup of lemon tea for Felicia and black coffee for Brandon.

Felicia sipped the steaming tea and observed the comfortable camaraderie Brandon seemed to have with the older ladies. They were all obviously taken with his easy charm.

"Brandon is doing such a fabulous job of getting this first show up and going," a dark-haired woman at the other end of the table gushed. "So many of the old company have come back just to work with him."

"And we've sold out the Opera House Ball," Lola announced. "We're getting calls and letters every day from people interested in donating to help reopen the theater. Everyone's so excited about having Brandon heading up the Opera House. Of course, we all want him to stay on permanently."

She cast a hopeful glance at Brandon. He smiled back in a noncommittal fashion.

"I knew we'd sell out the ball," Mrs. Parks put in, beaming at Brandon and Felicia. "With Brandon Donnelly and Felicia Marick on our side, we'll have the Opera House back on its feet in no time at all."

Her faded blue eyes sparkled happily. "So many young people aren't interested in their hometowns. They just leave and never come back. It's wonderful to see two young people who care about their roots and who want to give back to their hometown."

Felicia listened and smiled, but the conversation left her feeling oddly unsettled. Growing up, she'd never truly felt like she belonged, like Granbury was her town. She always felt like an outsider, dumped by her mother onto her grandmother. She'd felt rootless, despite her grandmother's loving care.

But these women seemed to assume that Felicia did belong in Granbury. It made her feel warm and cold at the same time.

She realized then that Lola must have asked her a question, but she hadn't heard it.

"Excuse me?"

"I said you must be looking forward to working with Brandon again," Lola repeated. "I remember seeing you two working together at the Opera House years ago."

"Oh, yes," Felicia said quietly, avoiding Brandon's gaze. But she felt the heat of his eyes beside her.

"I could see then that the two of you had talent. But, of course, I never expected you'd both go so far." Lola hesitated. "I'd hoped Dory—but, oh, well. She had other ideas." She looked around suddenly. "Dory was supposed to meet us here, too. Oh, there she is." Lola waved her arm.

Felicia turned. A slim, attractive woman with straight brown hair approached. Dory smiled, her rose-colored lips opening as she spotted her mother.

"Hi, Mom," Dory said, breathing quickly as if she'd hurried.

Felicia stood and stretched out her hand politely,

tamping down the nervous, edgy sensation in her stomach. Dory took her hand and shook it with a warm, light touch.

Brandon stood as well, and Dory took his hand next. He nodded at her and smiled. "Good to see you again," he said.

Dory settled in next to her mother.

"I'm really excited about working with you, Felicia," Dory said, her eyes glowing.

The honesty behind her admission floored Felicia. She hadn't known Dory very well in school. Dory had seemed aloof back then, a part of an old, established clique where Felicia had felt she had no place.

"I always tell everyone that I went to high school with you," Dory added. "It impresses people."

Felicia's eyes widened in surprise. Dory, voted Most Popular in high school, bragged about knowing the shy, insecure girl Felicia had been? Life suddenly seemed topsy-turvy. She'd always been so envious of Dory.

A laugh bubbled up from Felicia's throat, and Dory joined in.

"It's silly, I know," Dory said when the laughter stopped.

"Thank you," Felicia told her, still smiling. The strange, warm-cold feeling from earlier washed over her again. Here she was, back in Granbury, sharing a laugh with Dory Dunbar. It wasn't a scene she had ever envisioned.

She recalled that Brandon had given Dory the role of Angel in the show and the jealousy that she'd felt. She glanced at Brandon beside her. He was smiling at Dory.

Was he attracted to her?

The thought rushed on her from out of nowhere. She

pushed it back. That was ridiculous. It was none of her business, anyway.

Was that why he'd given Dory the part of Angel?

Felicia bit her lower lip, then tried to smile again as laughter and conversation swirled around her. Dory was grinning at Brandon, her dark eyes animated. Felicia cupped her hot mug of tea, struggling to steady the slight tremor of her hands.

Brandon, one arm relaxed over the back of his chair, noticed the shake of Felicia's fingers as she gripped her tea. She had just seemed to be growing comfortable, but now she was tense again.

He knew she was upset about playing Veronica in the show. Surely she wasn't angry with Dory. He was the one responsible for the casting.

Felicia was staring into her tea with a stiff smile pasted on her lips. The sweep of her black lashes against her butter-soft skin hid her eyes. Then her lashes flashed up, and she met Brandon's gaze. He sensed a silent, vulnerable darkness there, and then she blinked and turned away to look at Mrs. Parks.

Felicia's long blond curls swayed enticingly across her shoulders. A sudden, barely resistible yearning to reach out and run his fingers through her sunshine-gold hair tore at Brandon.

"I need to be going now," Felicia announced abruptly. "It's been so nice meeting all of you. I'll look forward to seeing you again tomorrow evening at the ball."

She stood quickly, picking up her script, and Brandon rose beside her. The ladies expressed assorted disappointed sounds.

"I'm okay," Felicia said to Brandon as he started after her.

"I'll walk you to your car."

"That's not necessary."

He smiled and took her arm.

"Goodbye, ladies," he said.

Felicia thought she saw him incline his head toward Dory.

"Bye, Brandon," Dory called. "Bye, Felicia."

When the shop door squeaked shut behind them, Felicia shook Brandon's arm roughly from hers.

"I don't need a bodyguard everywhere I go," she said with irritation. "I can walk to my car by myself, thank you. I'm sure the ladies would like you to stay."

He cocked a brow.

"I'm sure they would. But I prefer to walk you to your car."

Felicia gave a soft sigh.

"I don't want you to."

She spun around on her heel and started away, then Brandon reached out and pulled her back to him.

"Why are you so angry?" he demanded.

Felicia laughed harshly.

"Why am I angry?" she repeated sarcastically. "Oh, I don't know, Brandon. Could it be because you're trying to ruin my career?"

"I'm not trying to ruin your career."

Felicia sighed again, heavily. Frustration welled up in her chest. A keen headache stabbed behind her eyes.

"Look, forget it," she said tiredly. "I had a late night last night. I'm going home." She gave Brandon a hard stare. "But get this one thing straight, Brandon: I'm playing Veronica only because you're forcing my hand. You're not going to defeat me." Her eyes shot sparks at him as she ground the words out.

She flipped back around and strode toward the street. The square hummed with the mid-morning rush of shoppers and traffic. Felicia's mind roiled with the morning's events, and she stepped into the street carelessly, barely stumbling back in time to miss an approaching car.

Brandon's stomach turned over as he watched Felicia lurch backward. Covering the short distance quickly, he tugged Felicia against him, steadying her. She was breathing heavily, her heart tripping in her chest. He could feel the blood pounding in her veins. Her emerald eyes swept up to his, dark with fright.

Several bystanders had witnessed the near accident and had stopped to stare. Brandon tightened his hold on Felicia, realizing sharply what had almost occurred.

"Felicia—" he began.

She drew back, pushing his arms from her.

"I'm okay." She laughed shakily. "You seem to be making a habit of rescuing me today."

"I don't mind," Brandon told her softly.

"I do," she whispered.

A heavy truck roared by, then huffed to a halt at the corner stoplight. In the noise of its passing, Brandon swallowed the words he wished he could say, words that would change her into a trembling rabbit on the lawn at dusk, springing away from him forever.

He couldn't tell her that he still had feelings for her. Not yet.

Brandon sucked his breath in harshly as he watched Felicia warily cross the street to the courthouse parking lot, her blond tresses bobbing against her back, her hips swaying in an enchanting rhythm.

She took his breath away. After all these years, he still wanted her. More than ever.

Felicia rested, stomach down, on a long rubber raft just off the dock. Her grandmother's home was nestled alongside a peaceful cove that snaked away from the main lake, making it a tranquil place for lounging and swimming free from the disturbance of most recreational boaters.

She closed her eyes against the sun and dabbled one hand lazily in the lake. Brandon's face appeared before her eyes. Since she'd come back from town the day before, she'd been seething inside about Brandon's insulting insistence that she play Veronica.

Veronica—the best role for her. *Ha!* she scoffed inwardly. Brandon didn't know anything about her work if he thought that. She'd made a successful career of playing sweet innocents like Angel. The thought of the emotional angst of Veronica gnawed at Felicia's nerves. Playing a part like Veronica required delving into the experience of deep loss. She'd had enough of that in real life. She preferred the escape of Angel.

But she'd never get the part of Angel now. In the benefit show or in the film.

She'd tried to get in touch with Noreen right away. She would know how to put the proper spin control on the story before it got out of hand with the press. But she'd been able to do no more than leave a message with Noreen's office.

"Watch me, Mommy!" Robin called.

Felicia lifted her head and opened her eyes. Robin stood poised to jump from the dock, giggling excitedly. Libby relaxed in a deck chair nearby, sipping a tall glass of iced tea.

Robin flew through the air, plopping sloppily in the water and raining a shower of splashes over her mother. She rose sputtering from beneath the water, laughing joyfully. Sunlight glittered all around her.

At least Robin seemed to be having a good time, Felicia thought. Seeing her own daughter here, where she'd grown up, was an unsettling experience.

She wanted Robin to grow up happy and secure. But the fact was, Robin was virtually fatherless. Rodney was completely uninterested in his offspring.

The recollection of how much Brandon had once wanted children popped into her head. But he hadn't had any. He'd never married.

Felicia closed her eyes again and rested against the raft. She hadn't seen Brandon since the day before. After she'd come back from town, she and Libby had spent the afternoon grocery shopping, settling into the house, and making chocolate-chip cookies with Robin.

Today, with an early night under their belts, they all felt better. The lake had tempted them, and after a quick run to the local discount department store first thing in the morning, they'd sat down in the garage and blown up rubber rafts. Much laughter and struggle had accompanied this exercise before they were able to head for the water, rafts in tow.

Felicia had tried to shove all thoughts of Brandon from her mind. But last night when she'd laid her head against her grandmother's soft embroidered pillow, his eyes had floated into her dreams. And now, again, as she drifted in the water, she couldn't rid herself of him.

She knew she'd hurt him. But she would never have thought he would treat her this way. There was no doubt that he'd engineered her return to Granbury.

And the reasons for that were clear as a bell now, she thought grimly.

Revenge.

Felicia squeezed her eyes shut tighter. She wasn't going to think about it for the rest of the day, she determined.

"I'm taking Robin inside for lunch. You want some?" Libby called. Felicia looked up to see Robin clambering up the ladder to the dock, water streaming down her sides. "I promised Robin I'd make grilled cheese sandwiches."

"No, that's okay," Felicia said. "I'm not really hungry."

She stretched out comfortably. The patter of Libby and Robin's footsteps faded away and she heard the back door slam as they went inside. She was alone, with only the sighing of the wind over water and the cawing of birds.

Relax, she reminded herself. This was supposed to be part vacation.

The raft dipped and swayed with a drowsy cadence as the breeze ruffled the lake. Felicia began to doze, and the vision of Brandon's laughing sapphire eyes filtered into her subconscious thoughts. Dreamily, she remembered his firm touch and the strength in his thick arms when he'd pulled her against his warm chest.

She heard a splash and felt a surge of movement. Felicia opened her eyes. The water split open beside her and Brandon rose up, shaking water from his face, grinning at her.

"You're not going to burn, are you?" he asked. His eyes twinkled with the reflection of sun off the water.

FOUR

Felicia started up, almost toppled off her raft, then rested back quickly to rebalance herself.

"What are you doing here?" she demanded.

"Swimming."

Brandon reached out and grasped the edge of Felicia's raft with one hand, leaning back to float along beside her. His eyes lowered protectively in the bright sun, but his gaze remained fastened on Felicia. Her wheat-gold hair, damp and curly, was twisted up beside her neck, leaving her satiny tanned back exposed. The merest wisp of midnight-blue bikini strap crossed her back. Lower, a skimpy curve of blue material clung to her shapely derriere.

Brandon stifled the yearning to whip free the blue strap and smooth his hand along the creamy valley down the middle of her back to the enchanting rise below.

"Well, then go swim someplace else. Like by your own dock." Felicia glared at him.

"I like the company here," Brandon said, grinning

as he eyed the swell of breast visible above her bikini as Felicia shifted up onto her elbows. ‘‘I can see why directors have been so eager to put you in a bathing suit in every movie.’’

‘‘This isn’t a movie.’’

Brandon’s gaze narrowed and his expression grew serious. Bright daylight poured around them.

‘‘No. This isn’t a movie,’’ he agreed slowly.

He closed his eyes and floated quietly. Water beaded up on his shoulders. Sunlight glowed over his bronzed skin. Brandon had always possessed a powerful build, tall and muscular. The perfect leading man, Felicia thought wryly.

Only not for her. A perfect leading man for her didn’t exist. Felicia didn’t believe in happily ever afters.

Brandon opened his eyes at that moment and caught her staring. She looked away uncomfortably, embarrassed, and gazed out at the thickly wooded hillside across the cove. Dark birds flitted above the trees, swooping down quickly only to soar again.

She’d forgotten how beautiful it was in Granbury and how intoxicating the lush abundance of nature and animals could be. How intoxicating Brandon could be.

‘‘You’re very successful,’’ he said into the peaceful quiet. She turned to meet his eyes. ‘‘But I’ve been disappointed, Felicia. All I see in your work is a facade. It’s not the real Felicia. Not the Felicia I worked with at the Opera House.’’

She squinted down at Brandon beside her in the water. The rise of anger provoked by his comment stunned her momentarily. Who was he to make such a pronouncement on her career?

‘‘I don’t know what you think you know about my career,’’ she said, with careful emphasis on each word. Brandon floated along with his eyes closed again, as if he didn't hear her. "I'll have you know that a lot of hard work has gone into my success. It's not easy making it in Hollywood, you know."

Hearing the defensive hurt in her own voice, she hesitated, then continued coolly, "I don't know what gives you the right to make judgments about my career. You were never interested in seeing me successful. You wanted me to stay in Granbury and have babies, instead."

Brandon lazily raised one eyelid, then lowered it, stretching his long, lean body up toward the midday sun.

"That's not true," he answered calmly, unruffled by her anger. "I always thought you had it in you to be successful. And I've kept up with your career." He flipped over, then pulled up close again to her raft, water draining off his smooth muscular shoulders.

Felicia found herself examining the curves of muscle and bone, then drew her eyes, reluctantly, up to Brandon's face. Something about the gentle way he'd responded to her hard words caught at her heart, and her resentment dissipated.

He'd followed her career?

"You have?" she prompted.

Why did she want to hear more? she wondered. If he'd followed her career, it was only in the hopes that one day this moment would come, when he could use her career against her. When he could hurt her the way she'd hurt him.

His lashes were still damp from his dive into the lake. Long and black. He had lashes a woman would kill for, she thought.

"Of course I have," he was saying. He pulled the side of the raft up against his chest, his face so close to hers she wondered if the tingling heat she felt in her chest came from him or the sun above her. ''I didn't stop caring about you just because you left, Felicia. I worried about you.''

She felt herself softening.

He sounded sincere. Didn't he?

''You shouldn't have worried,'' she said. ''I was fine. I found a job right away.'' She grinned a trifle ruefully. ''Not acting, of course. But I did get a job waitressing, working my legs off at an all-night coffee shop. During the day I went on every audition in town, I think.''

''It didn't take you long to get a part, though,'' he said.

''No,'' Felicia agreed. ''Not long. Just luck, I guess. I got that little part in *Meet the Morning*. I only had three lines. But Rodney was starring in that, and so . . .''

She let the explanation trail off. The tremor of movement in Brandon's cheek made her feel awkward, self-conscious.

''I didn't marry him to get ahead,'' she blurted out suddenly.

Brandon stared at her.

''Did I say that?'' he asked simply. Then, gently, as if to put her at ease, he added, ''I saw you in *Meet the Morning*. Those were the best three lines in the movie.''

Brandon grinned mischievously, daring her to laugh with him. And so she did.

''Sure,'' she said, smiling and finding herself relaxing in his company in spite of herself. ''I was ready for them. 'Do you want coffee?' 'Here's your coffee' and 'Let me know if you need anything else.' '' She raised her face up to the soothing rays of the early-afternoon sun. ''I think I was practicing those lines enough in my real life to swing them in a film. No rehearsal required."

For a quiet moment, sharing a piece of her life, she remembered what it had been like to be close to Brandon. Memories warmed over her of the hours they'd spent romping out in the lake, or swaying languidly on Grandmother's back-porch swing, drinking tart, chilly lemonade and laughing about little incidents that had happened the night before during the Opera House show.

And then, of course, those endless summer nights under the stars, making love on a quilt on the ground. Felicia bit her lower lip, the memories stinging her eyes.

"How are your parents?" she asked abruptly. Her thoughts were moving her into dangerous territory. She couldn't forget that he wanted to hurt her, was trying to damage her career.

His parents were a safe topic. Jake and Betty Donnelly had been, in many respects, the parents Felicia had never had. While they were growing up, Brandon had been too busy with sports and friends, and later college, to pay much attention to Felicia, four years his junior. But his parents had treated her like another daughter. In consideration of her grandmother's age, the Donnellys had taken it upon themselves to take their young neighbor under their wing in some ways.

Jake Donnelly had taught Felicia to swim and canoe and water-ski, right along with his daughter, Joanie, who was only two years older than Felicia. For her part, Betty Donnelly had shown Felicia how to apply makeup and dress more fashionably when Felicia was in high school, and even taught her to dance.

It was not until the summer Brandon returned to Granbury, after he'd graduated from college, that he had noticed Felicia. Noticed that she wasn't a child anymore.

"They're doing great," Brandon was saying. "They both retired, and they just wanted to be with their grandchildren, like I was telling you yesterday morning. So they moved to Savannah to be near Joanie and her family."

The referral to the incident at dawn the day before reinforced the reality of the present against the past. Eight years had passed since she and Brandon had been in love and Felicia had been like a member of the Donnelly family. She and Brandon couldn't return to that summer.

"I should go in," Felicia said. She paddled lightly with her hands, pushing the raft away from Brandon and back toward the dock. After plunging into the sun-warmed lake, she rose up and pulled herself onto the steps to the dock, dragging the raft up after her. As she pulled the raft onto the dock, she saw Brandon hauling himself up the ladder on the other side.

He stood beside her, dripping onto the wooden planks, wearing a brief red swimsuit. He gazed at her with an appreciative eye. Unnervingly appreciative, Felicia thought. She'd forgotten to carry a towel down to the dock with her, and she regretted it now. But, of course, she hadn't known Brandon would be following her into the water. Her bikini covered her in all the required places, but its French cut didn't leave any more to the imagination than was absolutely necessary.

Abandoning the raft on the dock, she stepped barefoot onto the soft green lawn. Brandon followed her with his eyes, watching the soft swing of her bare hips, her smooth tan glowing in the golden shimmer of afternoon. He smiled, watching the provocative movement of her long, slim legs.

Brandon hurried to catch up with her, coming up so close beside her that he brushed against her arm as they walked.

"I would think you would be awfully busy at the Opera House," Felicia said, without turning to look him in the face. "Even on the weekends. Surely there are more useful things you could be accomplishing than appointing yourself my guardian."

Her profile, delicate and well-formed, revealed no expression.

"Walking you home is my pleasure," Brandon responded with good humor. "Everything's under control with the Opera House. I'm more interested in seeing how my new star is doing."

Felicia stopped at that and swiveled to look at him.

"I'm not your 'new' star," she said. "In fact, I'm not your 'new' anything. This is just temporary. Very temporary."

"Of course," he said with a shrug. He was infuriating her, and for the moment, that was better than no reaction at all. He grinned boyishly.

Libby opened the door as they approached, and Robin ran out under her arm.

"Hi, Brandon!" Robin cried happily, obviously delighted to see him. She scurried to the top porch step and waited for Felicia and Brandon.

Brandon smiled broadly and Robin ran up to him, giggling. Felicia observed her daughter's behavior with wonder. Robin, usually reserved with strangers and isolated at home with Libby so much of the time, was clearly drawn to Brandon.

"Why don't I get everybody some iced tea?" Libby suggested, eyeing Brandon's nearly bare figure. She smiled questioningly at Felicia.

With the word *no* on the edge of Felicia's tongue, Robin piped up eagerly.

"Oh, yes, Mommy." She whipped around to gaze up at her mother. "Can we ask Brandon to stay?" Robin turned back to Brandon. "Me and Mommy and Libby made cookies last night. Do you want one?"

"What kind of cookies? Are they any good?" Brandon asked in a teasing voice.

"Oh, yes," Robin assured him. "They're chocolate chip. My favorite. I make good cookies, don't I, Mommy?"

"Yes, sweetheart, you make excellent cookies." Felicia looked around at the three of them. Brandon was settling into the porch swing, and Robin skipped up to jump onto the seat beside him. Libby, with a quick nod to Felicia, disappeared back into the house, presumably on her way to make iced tea and bring out the cookies.

It seemed they had all decided that Brandon was practically a part of the household. The situation seemed completely out of control, as if the world were hanging slightly askew.

Not so long ago, she had never thought she'd see Brandon again. And she hadn't wanted to see him again.

Well, maybe not entirely true, she admitted to herself as she watched Brandon rock the swing, listening to Robin's playful chatter.

Had she wanted to see Brandon again? Had a part of her hoped she'd see him, needed to see him again? After all, their relationship had no closure. It had ended abruptly with her departure.

That was it, she decided. If—and that was just an if—she had subconsciously hoped she'd see Brandon if she came back to Granbury, it was only because she needed closure. She felt guilty for never saying goodbye.

It certainly couldn't be because she still wanted him.

Certainly not.

And he certainly didn't want her. He was toying with her, playing games with her.

Brandon looked up from Robin and furrowed his brow as he met Felicia's eyes. She forced herself to ease away the frown that had settled on her face as she watched them. She turned and went inside.

Libby was in the kitchen pouring tea into tall, ice-filled glasses.

"I would have stayed outside if I'd known he'd be coming out to swim," Libby said when Felicia entered the kitchen. "He's such a dish. Did you get a load of him in that bathing suit? Enough to make your toes all curly. Do you think he likes me?"

"I wouldn't know," Felicia said, fingering the dewy moisture on one of the glasses.

"I can't believe you get to work with him every day at the Opera House," Libby said, her voice filled with soft envy. "You're so lucky."

Felicia hadn't shared with Libby her suspicions that Brandon had placed her in the role of Veronica in order to hurt her career. There was no use trying to make Libby understand. She was too enamored with Brandon to take Felicia's concerns seriously.

"Yeah. Real lucky." Felicia tried to smile.

Libby looked up at her and frowned.

"What's wrong, Felicia?"

"Nothing's wrong. Why would you think something's wrong?"

Libby drew her brows together. "I don't know. You just seem different. Worried or something."

Felicia shook her head.

"I guess I'm still a little tired, that's all," she told Libby.

"You're not mad about me liking Brandon? Because if you are—I mean, you had him first—"

"Libby! You don't 'have' people. Brandon and I knew each other a long time ago. A very long time ago. That's it."

The kitchen was quiet for a moment, and the sounds of Robin's laughter filtered in from the back porch.

"Okay." Libby carefully balanced three glasses of tea between her hands and headed for the back door. "Would you bring the cookies when you come out?" she called.

When she was gone, Felicia picked up the phone and dialed her agent's number. Noreen's machine picked up once again, and this time Felicia hung up without leaving a message.

Great time for Noreen to take a vacation, she thought.

She needed to talk to Noreen. Nobody knew yet about the casting at the Opera House, and she wanted to discuss it with Noreen before it got out. Felicia was certain there would be press at the opening of *Passion's Pride*. Some press might even show up while they were still in rehearsal.

Since the story had been printed mentioning Felicia's name as one of several actresses who were in the running for the movie role of Angel, there were bound to be questions about why Felicia wasn't playing the part. Questions that could be damaging.

Where was Noreen when she needed her?

Felicia trailed back to the bedroom and changed into a pair of blue jean shorts and a lace-edged white cotton top. Back in the kitchen, she loaded a paper plate with

Robin's chocolate-chip cookies and carried it and her own glass of tea out back.

Felicia heard laughter ringing merrily out on the shady porch as she pushed open the screen door. Brandon and Robin still sat on the porch swing, and Libby had slouched down onto the top step.

"Mommy, Brandon said he'd take me fishing," Robin said as Felicia stepped out onto the porch. Felicia set the cookies down on a little iron table, giving Brandon a hard look. "I can, can't I?" her daughter begged.

"Brandon's been telling us about his boat," Libby told Felicia. "It's his parents', really, but they keep it here so they can fish whenever they come up for vacation." She turned to Brandon, "I love to fish. It's so relaxing."

Felicia choked on her tea and had to set her glass down on the table while she overcame her coughing.

Libby loved to fish?

"Are you okay?" Brandon inquired solicitously.

"I'm fine," Felicia said when she could. She sat down on the step next to Libby, turning her gaze on the sun-splashed lake. A light breeze rippled through the blue water, pushing along a family of geese that scooted beside the shore. Farther down the way, she saw a long, shiny blue boat bobbing in the slip of Brandon's dock.

She looked back up at Brandon. He was munching into a chocolate-chip cookie under Robin's watchful eye.

"Delicious!" he raved, smiling at the five-year-old beside him. Robin beamed.

The easy way Robin responded to Brandon bothered Felicia. She wasn't accustomed to seeing Robin take to strangers so easily. Brandon exuded an effortless rapport with the little girl. Felicia recalled how much he used to talk about having children.

She wondered why he'd never married and had any.

"When did you first leave Granbury for New York?" Felicia asked suddenly.

Brandon turned his cobalt-blue eyes to hers, his expression hidden in the shadows of the porch.

"About a year after you left," he said. Soon after he'd heard Felicia had married Rodney Kent, he added silently to himself. It was only then that it struck home to him what a fool he'd been to think she'd come back, to think she loved him.

"Oh." Felicia sighed, turning away as if she didn't know what else to say.

Her golden hair nestled in damp tendrils against her neck. Brandon longed to reach out and move her hair and brush his fingers up to her satiny cheek. Her face was lightly flushed from the afternoon under the cloudless sky, adding a pink sheen to her sunny tan.

She acted friendly one minute and distant the next, he thought with frustration. She backed away whenever the conversation got too close.

"It wasn't the same here without you," Brandon said, noticing with satisfaction that his comment brought her head swiveling back to face him. "I missed you."

Felicia's heart began to thump.

"Really?" she couldn't help prodding.

Brandon nodded. "You were the most talented actress the Opera House had. After you left, it just wasn't the same."

Felicia's heart thudded to a stop. Why did she keep getting these bizarre, ridiculous notions that he'd truly loved her back then? He'd missed her abilities at the Opera House, not her.

She'd fallen for him that summer, that one hot,

humid season after she'd finished high school. But he'd wanted to tie her down, to hold her back, to keep her in Granbury. She could easily have ended up like her own mother—alone, with a child, and no means of financial support.

Glancing over at Robin, she realized sadly that she had ended up alone with a child after all. But at least she had her career. She could support her daughter. She'd never abandon Robin the way she'd been abandoned.

She'd put her career first. It had been the right decision. She watched as Robin pressed another cookie on Brandon as soon as he finished his first one.

"These are great," he told the little girl. Robin smiled wide and bit into her own cookie. Brandon swallowed and rocked the swing slowly in the fresh breeze. "I sure do miss this town when I'm in New York. It's great to be back." He shot a narrowed glance at Felicia. "I may stay on permanently as the managing director up at the Opera House."

"Well, I think this place is tons better than L.A.," Libby said into the silence that followed. "It's so smoggy there, and the beaches are totally crowded. I haven't seen even one boat out on this cove yet," she added.

"I think it's neat here, too," Robin said. She jumped up from the swing and ran over to Felicia, flinging her arms around her neck. "You never said if I could go fishing with Brandon, Mommy. Can I? Please! I want to learn to fish."

Felicia longed to say no.

She didn't want Brandon getting involved with her daughter, getting too close.

But she saw the need in Robin, the need for a relationship with a male figure. A father figure. Rodney was certainly a sorry example. He'd virtually ignored

Robin since her birth. Felicia and Rodney had separated shortly after Robin was born, but initially Felicia had been eager for Rodney to continue as a part of his daughter's life. But he hadn't been interested, and as time went on, Felicia was glad. She knew Rodney's fast lifestyle was a bad example for an impressionable child.

Still, she knew Robin was losing something she needed.

But Brandon? Could she allow him to become close to Robin when it would last only a matter of weeks?

"Please, Mommy."

Robin's round hazel eyes held an imploring quality that Felicia found hard to resist.

"I'll take good care of her," Brandon assured her.

Felicia met his eyes. His gaze was gentle, caring. She knew he wouldn't hurt her child. He might want to hurt her, but Brandon loved children. Of that, at least, Felicia was sure.

"I'll be there, too, of course," Libby chimed in. Her face spread in a brilliant smile to Brandon.

"Okay," Felicia said, relenting. She pushed off the niggle of annoyance that Libby's eager, fawning attitude toward Brandon sparked. If Libby wanted him, she could have him.

"Great," Brandon said. "Then it's a date. Tomorrow morning, six A.M. sharp."

Libby's happy expression momentarily faltered, but she recovered quickly.

"I'll make you breakfast," she offered to Brandon, brightening.

"Libby," Felicia said, "why don't you grab some bread inside and take Robin down to feed those geese?"

Libby seemed as if she was about to protest, but Felicia sent her a stern glance and Libby went inside to get some bread. She came back out and Robin gleefully skipped after her nanny toward the lakeshore.

Felicia quietly watched her daughter tossing bread crumbs at the loudly honking geese for several minutes, then stood up and turned to Brandon.

"What's going on?" Felicia demanded. "Why are you making such a point of involving yourself in my personal life?"

"I don't know what you're talking about," Brandon replied with the consistently effortless composure that grated on Felicia's nerves.

Not to mention his insistence on looking so incredibly sexy, she thought with irritation. If he wasn't dripping onto her den floor in his underwear, he was draped on her porch swing in his swimsuit. In both cases, he reminded her in no uncertain terms of his powerful physique, his smooth tanned skin, his crisply curling chest hair. . . .

"You do, too!" she shot back, more angrily than she'd meant to.

"I'm your neighbor, remember?" he said. "Where do you expect me to be when I'm not at the Opera House?"

She didn't have a good answer for that, so she ignored the question.

"Look, I know how you feel about me," she said. "I know what's going on with the show and why you're giving me the role of Veronica. I can handle it. I'm used to working hard and fighting for my career. That's how I got where I am." She crossed her arms tightly across her chest. "But Robin is just a child. A young, impressionable child. I don't want you playing games with her. Don't try to hurt me through Robin. We'll only be here until the show's over, and then we'll be gone. She'll never see you again. If you get too close to her, it will only hurt her when we leave."

Brandon stood up and strode over to Felicia. The shadows of the porch left his eyes dark and unreadable. Felicia unconsciously backed up a step until she brushed against the porch rail. Brandon followed her, staring down into her eyes. He reached up and touched her cheek, pushing back a stray tendril of hair.

He couldn't resist touching her any longer, and the passionate fire in her eyes as she'd shot out the flurry of angry words drew him like a magnet. Anger was the only honest emotion he believed she'd shown him since her return to Granbury.

The soft caress of Brandon's fingers against Felicia's skin seemed to shock her, and she jerked back from his hand. He let his hand fall to his side, but he didn't move away. Somewhere in the distance the joyful laughter of her child floated in the air.

"Is that what you're afraid of?" Brandon asked, his voice a husky whisper. "Being close?"

Felicia felt his eyes penetrating as if to her very soul. She flinched away farther.

"No," she whispered in return. She skirted along the porch rail, putting a safe distance between herself and Brandon. "I just want to be sure you understand that Robin is vulnerable. Be careful with her."

He turned, following her with his eyes.

"Of course," he agreed. "I would never try to hurt her."

She knew in her heart that he was telling her the truth.

"I'll see you tonight," Brandon added softly. "I'll pick you up at seven."

Felicia frowned.

"I can drive myself to the Opera House Ball," she said.

"You shouldn't arrive alone," Brandon objected. "You're the special guest of honor. The Opera board asked me to bring you since we live next door to each other."

"That was very thoughtful," Felicia persisted. "But I know my way around town, and I have my own car. Thank you, anyway."

She crossed the porch and opened the screen door, turning at the sound of Brandon's voice.

"It would be terrible if there was speculation that we'd had a falling out and you'd refused to attend the ball with me," he murmured. "It might seem terribly strange, don't you think? Since we live next door and all."

He shrugged.

"But," he continued, "like you said, you're used to that kind of negative attention."

He casually stepped off the porch, turning back to Felicia as he moved into the sunshine of the afternoon.

"Seven's okay, then?" he asked.

Felicia slammed the door.

FIVE

"Ooo, pretty, Mommy," Robin cooed from the couch as her mother entered the den at seven o'clock that evening.

"Yes, very pretty," came a deeper voice. "Downright gorgeous."

Felicia flipped around, surprised, and spotted Brandon coming around the corner from the kitchen. He held a glass, and Felicia guessed Libby had been plying him with iced tea again. Clearly, he was determined to drive her to the Opera House Ball.

Brandon glanced down at his watch.

"And so punctual," he said, looking back up at Felicia and smiling. "It's exactly seven o'clock. To think I had expected to have to wait for you."

Felicia ignored him and instead turned her attention to her young daughter. She bent down and kissed Robin's cheek.

"You be good," Felicia said. "I'll see you in the morning."

"I'm going fishing in the morning, remember, Mommy?"

"Yes," Felicia said, restraining a sigh. "I remember."

She told Libby goodbye, and Brandon followed her outside. As they made their way down the walk in silence, he relished every inch of her sophisticated appearance.

She'd obviously prepared for the Opera House Ball with meticulous care, choosing a slinky dark rose dress that fell in straight, sleek lines along her figure. Brandon had noticed immediately the way the plunging V neckline hugged the curve of her full breasts, down to her slim waist and hips, ending several inches above her knees. Her small feet were encased in high-heeled shoes that matched the exact rose shade of her dress.

Her honey-colored hair was brushed upward and fastened casually atop her head with a gold clip, allowing recalcitrant blond strands to fall down about her shoulders in sensuous disarray. The tumbling locks begged touching, and the thought of giving in to that invitation sent hot surges radiating through Brandon's bloodstream.

His sedan was parked at the curb, and before Felicia could open the door to her rented Mercedes, Brandon slipped his hand beneath her elbow and guided her gently to the street. She shot a warning glance at him when he touched her, but when he opened the passenger door of his vehicle expectantly, she merely shrugged and sighed.

It was only a car ride, Felicia thought as she sat down. She'd shake him when they got to the ball.

"Just for the record, I'm not in the habit of being pushed around," Felicia told him when he opened the driver's side and eased in beside her. "Don't take too seriously the fact that I'm going along with you on this."

Brandon cocked his brows with a dark flicker of movement.

"I wouldn't dream of taking you seriously, Felicia," he murmured. He smiled, then keyed the ignition. The car gently hummed to life.

The obnoxious self-assurance in his grin grated against Felicia's already raw nerves. She wanted to spout something angry about the way he'd said he didn't take her seriously, but since she'd been the one to instruct him against doing exactly that, she couldn't think of anything to say.

Brandon darted another quick glance at Felicia.

"You look beautiful," he said into the silence.

"We don't have to talk," Felicia said, cutting him off. She stared out the window.

"Have you taken time to study the play yet?" Brandon asked, persisting as if she hadn't said a thing.

Felicia whirled on him.

"Yes, I have," she replied hotly. "Enough to confirm that my sense of Veronica as a rotten part is correct. Angel has all the good scenes."

Brandon shook his head.

"Not so," he disagreed. "What about the scene where Veronica confronts Stefan about his affair with Angel—that he's been trying to hide from Veronica?"

"That's a good scene? I may need a whole truckload of onions to get through it."

Brandon's lips shifted upward slightly.

"I doubt that'll be necessary," he said. "You've got it in you, Felicia."

"I don't want to have it in me," she countered. "Angel has the fun lines. She's charming and vivacious. Veronica has all the emotional baggage."

"It's high time you stopped playing fluff roles." The words came out flat and serious.

"Fluff roles!"

Brandon turned the wheel sharply as he rounded a

curve. When the road straightened out again, he glanced at Felicia. Her eyes flashed brightly at him in the golden evening sun.

"That's right. Fluff roles."

"I don't play fluff."

"What do you call it?"

Felicia was silent for a moment. How dare he challenge her about her career? But for a reason she couldn't fathom, she felt compelled to make him understand.

"Happy," she said after thinking several moments. "I like to play happy people in happy movies."

Brandon shook his head.

"I don't think so," he disagreed. "You play simple, one-dimensional characters. Fluff. Roles that don't require any emotional investment on your part." He waited a few seconds, then continued. "But I know you have a keen sense of theatrics, a powerful dramatic talent. Why don't you use it?"

"What difference does it make?" Felicia demanded.

Brandon sent her a hard, penetrating glance.

"It makes a lot of difference," he told her. "Talent should never be wasted. Especially if it's being wasted simply because you're afraid to use it."

Felicia's chin jutted forward.

"Afraid? That's ridiculous." She turned away and stared through the window at the wooded countryside speeding by outside. "You don't know me at all, Brandon. You don't know anything about me. Just because a long time ago we . . . just because we used to be . . ."

"What? Used to be what?" Brandon challenged.

Felicia swiveled to face him again and his gaze flew to hers, defying her to look away.

"The word is *lovers*, Felicia."

The darkness in his indigo eyes held her until he forced his attention back to the road by necessity.

"You haven't forgotten that we were lovers, have you, Felicia?" His voice came to her quietly but with a rough edge. His chiseled profile in the gleaming late-day sun looked hard, unyielding. It wasn't the voice of a lover.

"How can I forget?" Felicia demanded. "You won't stop reminding me." She shifted, the tension in her legs beginning a slow, aching pulsation.

"Really?" Brandon turned a suggestive perusal over Felicia. "I believe this is the first time I've mentioned it. Maybe you're the one who can't stop thinking about our past together."

Felicia felt an embarrassed blush creeping up her neck. He'd neatly twisted her words to make it sound like she was the one stuck in the past. She wished she'd driven her own car to the ball. She even wished she'd brought Libby and Robin with her to run interference. But she didn't like to bring Robin out in the public eye any more than necessary, so she'd decided to keep her home.

"This whole conversation is completely nonsensical," Felicia said coolly. She firmly placed her gaze on the verdant landscape outside the car window and determined to ignore Brandon if he tried to speak to her again.

But, of course, he didn't give her the chance. He didn't try to strike up conversation again, and they drove in frigid silence until he pulled up in front of the tall, white-columned country club.

He handed his car keys to a parking attendant and slipped his arm gallantly through Felicia's, as easily as if they were lovers still. She started to pull away but stopped when she realized the firm grip he had on her arm would require a crowbar to remove.

"Smile," Brandon said in a low, warning tone as they moved through the open doors. "Show me all that 'happy' stuff you're so good at."

Felicia stifled the caustic response she wanted to make, deciding that continuing to ignore Brandon was her best course. She looked brightly around the lobby, determined to find some way to enjoy the evening in spite of Brandon.

Scattered groupings of guests dotted the entry, holding long-stemmed glasses of bubbling champagne, talking and laughing softly. Several people turned and smiled at Felicia and Brandon, waving warmly.

"Brandon! Felicia!"

They turned in unison to find Lola swooping across the floor toward them, her voluminous purple ballgown flying out around her. She descended on them like a bird falling on its hapless prey.

"Thank goodness you're here," Lola cried when she reached them, as excited as if there had been some doubt as to whether they would appear at the ball. "The television people are here from the Atlanta stations. They're setting up in the ballroom, and they want to interview the two of you before the evening starts, if possible. They want to get back to the city before the late news."

Lola slipped between them, breaking Brandon's hold on Felicia's arm with the force of her enthusiasm.

"Isn't it lovely? That's what we get with celebrities, you see," Lola continued as she steered Brandon and Felicia into the ballroom. "This is going to be great coverage for the Opera House. We'd probably be lucky to get print coverage without you two. Oh, that reminds me. Reporters from the Atlanta newspapers are here, too. And, of course, we have our local people from the *Granbury Globe*. But they're easy—they already love you. You're hometown folk. It's the city people we have to work on."

Hometown folk. That notion of belonging always made Felicia feel uneasy. She knew already she was going to feel like a fraud before the evening was out, pretending that she was just a good old Granbury girl.

But telling everybody what an outsider she really was wouldn't do the Opera House any good, she reminded herself.

They entered the ballroom through double doors, and Felicia withheld a gasp of delight at the glitter of soft lights and gleaming tableware. The long, tall-ceilinged room was filled with crimson cloth-covered tables set with sparkling china and glass. One table was situated sideways on a slightly raised dais with a podium. A screen was set up behind the podium.

Lola hesitated in the doorway. They could see the TV crews across the room, studying their angle on the podium as they positioned their equipment.

"We're going to have a slide show to go along with a short history of the Opera House," Lola explained. "I'll handle that and say a few additional words about our plans for reopening the Opera House. You wouldn't mind saying a few words, would you?"

Lola raised her brows at Felicia and Brandon.

"I—I don't know what I'd say," Felicia began. She swallowed nervously. She detested speaking at public events. Despite her career as an actress, she found herself shy when faced with public appearances—the kind of appearances that didn't come with a script.

"You don't have to say much, dear," Lola told her, squeezing her arm in encouragement. "But everyone would be so disappointed if you didn't say anything at all. Just tell everyone how happy you are to be home, and how much the Opera House means to you. That's all."

Felicia chewed her bottom lip.

"Okay," she agreed reluctantly.

"Count me in," Brandon said, smiling. He could see Felicia was nervous about speaking at the ball, and an idea popped into his head suddenly. There might be a way he could show her how much he wanted to help her, rather than hurt her. He moved around Lola, drawing his arm away from hers and stepping to Felicia. He picked up her hand and covered it with his. "I suggest Felicia and I go to the podium together. It would save time," he said, then with a wink at Lola added, "and the crowd would love to see us together. There are a lot of people who'll remember us from our days together at the Opera House."

"That's a fabulous idea," Lola gushed, pleased with the plan.

Brandon caught Felicia's eyes, and in their sea-green depths he saw a softening, a tentative gratitude. He pressed his fingers against her hand. Of everyone at the ball tonight, he was probably the only one who knew that at heart Felicia was very shy.

"Felicia Marick, Brandon Donnelly, I'm Shana Williams," came a businesslike voice behind them. They turned to see a conservatively dressed, attractive woman who quickly introduced herself as the entertainment reporter from an Atlanta television station. "Would you mind giving me a short interview on tape that we can use tonight on the eleven o'clock news?"

In no time, Felicia and Brandon found themselves standing in front of the cameraman, answering a spate of direct questions. Felicia admired the easy way Brandon relaxed in front of the camera, as natural as if he'd been born to it. While she, a regular performer in films, felt jumpy as a novice.

"Now I've been told that you two had more than a stage partnership in the past," Shana Williams said after finishing up her line of questions dealing with the Opera House benefit. "Is there a chance of any romance blooming over at the Granbury Opera House?"

Brandon laughed and placed his arm casually over Felicia's shoulders.

"I'm sure there's plenty of romance in Granbury," he told the reporter. He turned and smiled at Felicia, then looked back at Shana Williams. "And Felicia and I have always been great friends."

"Have you kept in contact over the years since you both became successful?" the reporter questioned, turning her eye on Felicia.

"No, we haven't," Felicia answered simply.

"We've kept up with each other's careers," Brandon interjected.

"Well, which is it?" Shana Williams persisted. "Have you or haven't you?"

"Haven't," Felicia clarified.

"Have," Brandon said at the same time.

Felicia kicked him with a tiny, barely concealed flip of her high-heeled foot.

"Ouch," Brandon said, and laughed. He hugged Felicia against his side. He felt her trying to pull away, so he gave her a quick peck on the cheek with his lips. "It's just like old times," he told the reporter. "Old friends are the best."

The reporter smiled, then her eyes narrowed on Felicia.

"I understand you'll be performing in *Passion's Pride*," Shana Williams said. "Are you preparing for the film role by any chance? It's been reported that producer Howard Huberts is considering you for the film.''

Felicia's chest stiffened. She had to force herself to speak, to act natural.

''This has nothing to do with the upcoming film,'' Felicia told her firmly. She drew her lips up into a strained smile. ''I'm just here to perform in a benefit for the Granbury Opera House.''

Thankfully, the reporter accepted Felicia's explanation and gestured to the cameraman to shut off the machine. She thanked Brandon and Felicia, then stepped back to allow the other two TV crews their opportunity to interview the pair.

After them came the newspaper reporters. They scribbled quickly, barely glancing up as they shot out their questions. Lola hovered around Brandon and Felicia during the interviewing, ready to step in to pitch the Opera House whenever she spied an opening.

Felicia exhaled a sigh of relief as the last reporter slapped shut his pad and thanked the three of them. The ballroom was filling with benefit attendees, arriving and settling in their places with much chatter and tinkling of wineglasses. A tall, thin, silver-haired man with a camera dangling from a strap around his neck approached, causing Lola to leap to her feet.

''Felicia, Brandon, you must meet Wilbur Barron, the editor of the *Granbury Globe*,'' Lola told them.

Felicia and Brandon shook hands in turn with the editor of Granbury's twice-weekly newspaper.

''Wilbur's been giving us the most lovely coverage for our reopening,'' Lola said. ''We can always count on our local paper, can't we, Wilbur?''

Wilbur slung his arm around Lola's back and hugged her lightly before turning his attention to Brandon and Felicia. He pulled a pad and pen out of his back pocket.

"How long have you been in town?" Wilbur asked Felicia.

"Just since late Thursday night," Felicia told him.

"How does it feel to be working with Brandon Donnelly again?" Wilbur asked. "I bet I can pull some old photos from our files from when you two worked at the Opera House eight years ago. Are you looking forward to working together again?"

Felicia glanced at Brandon. His lips opened in a gentle grin. She remembered the tingle of his lips brushing ever so tenderly against her cheek during the earlier interview.

She forced her gaze back to the Granbury editor.

"Uh, yes," she fumbled.

"I'm thrilled to be working with Felicia again," Brandon said.

"What does it mean to you to be able to help the Opera House this way?" Wilbur questioned, turning to Brandon.

"This opportunity means a lot to me," Brandon told him. "I've missed . . . Granbury a great deal." His eyes were pulled inexorably to Felicia. "Those were great times, starting out on the Opera House stage."

Wilbur glanced back and forth between Felicia and Brandon, a subtle grin lifting his mouth.

"There was some romance going on between the two of you back then," Wilbur said. "Any chance that—"

"No." Felicia surprised herself with the ferocity with which the denial sprang from her lips.

She felt a touch on her shoulder and turned to find Lola bending forward.

"I think we'd better be seated," Lola said quietly.

Wilbur stuck his pad and pen back in his pocket.

"Can I get with you Monday for a full interview?" he asked, eyeing Brandon and Felicia hopefully.

"Absolutely," Brandon agreed, shaking Wilbur's hand vigorously. "Come on down to the Opera House anytime. We'll be there."

Felicia gave Wilbur a stiff smile, glad to have been rescued before she'd been forced to continue the interview at that point. She hoped that Wilbur would have forgotten the topic they'd broken off on by the time Monday rolled around.

"Nothing like Granbury people helping Granbury people," Mayor Richard Foley said as he swung Felicia slowly around the dance floor. A band played softly behind them. "We're lucky to have you and Brandon."

A tightness swelled in Felicia's throat.

"Thank you," she said self-consciously.

"Lots of folks get too big for their britches and forget all about where they came from," the Granbury mayor continued. "But you're a hometown girl at heart, aren't you?"

"Yes," Felicia said, a crack in her voice. "How many years have you been mayor here?" she asked quickly, changing the subject.

She couldn't bear to hear one more word about how dedicated she was to Granbury. So many people had come up to her during the evening, thanking her for helping with the reopening, sharing a faded memory of her grandmother, telling Felicia which of her movies they'd seen.

They all made her feel like a fraud, just like she'd anticipated when the evening had started. Why did they all think she belonged? She wasn't born in Granbury. She'd just been dumped there by her mother on a grandmother ill-equipped to raise an energetic child.

Felicia hadn't had active, young parents to take her to and fro for school activities, to socialize with other parents of children her age, to give her a home where she felt secure. Her grandmother's friends were elderly, her interests had been sedate. If it hadn't been for the kindness of Jake and Betty Donnelly, Felicia would have rarely left her grandmother's yard after school.

She definitely hadn't felt like she belonged in Granbury. She had known she didn't belong there, had known she had parents elsewhere who'd abandoned her.

Felicia's problem had been that she didn't belong anywhere. And she still didn't.

But since she'd returned to Granbury, everyone acted as if she was a native of the town. They treated her like a hometown girl made good, someone they were proud of claiming as their own.

The applause had vibrated in the air when she and Brandon had approached the ballroom podium after Lola's introduction. The sea of clapping hands and welcoming smiles had left Felicia overwhelmed, teary even. She'd been grateful for Brandon's presence by her side. Felicia had done little more than thank the crowd for attending, and an uproar of renewed applause had rung out.

Brandon had slipped his arm around her waist and joked with the audience about changes in the town and local politics. It amazed Felicia that Brandon already seemed to have a handle on all the inside political gossip that made grist for light humor.

He had a way of making everyone comfortable. Everyone except her.

She looked over Mayor Foley's shoulder, searching for Brandon. She found him across the dim room, dancing with a woman she quickly identified as Dory. Brandon bent his head to her, listening closer to hear something Dory said, then smiling down at her.

A twist of pure jealousy snaked through Felicia's abdomen. She inhaled a quick, deep breath, determined to tame the unwelcome feeling. It annoyed her that she seemed utterly unable to control her emotions since her return to Granbury.

"I'm sorry, you must be exhausted," Mayor Foley said considerately. "I know you've danced with everyone in town tonight." He smiled kindly, his bald pate gleaming pinkly in the soft lights. "You should sit down. I'll bring you a glass of water."

"Thank you," Felicia said, grateful for the man's thoughtfulness. She was tired. The last few days had been incredibly full.

The mayor guided her through the open garden doors to the long veranda that swept across the back of the plantation-style country club.

"You rest here where it's quiet," he told her and disappeared.

Felicia settled into a chair, then rose again and wandered to the railing to look down over the lawn. A fragrant breeze nipped at her cheeks, bringing a welcome cooling to her warm skin.

Below, she saw a couple embracing in the gazebo on the lawn. She glanced away, her eyes straying over the veranda. Several couples wandered casually near the far end of the deck, then turned and disappeared inside through another door. When she looked down to the lawn again, the couple in the gazebo had vanished as well. She was alone. She trailed away from the ballroom doors into the shadows of the veranda.

She stopped and leaned against the railing, closing her eyes for a second, inhaling the fresh air—so different from the smoggy air in L.A.—and breathed in the soft scent of summer in Georgia. Music and laughter floated softly over her from the ballroom in the distance.

The music, the laughter, the breeze, all seemed to meld together. The skin on the back of her neck tingled with a light sensation that intermingled with the wind.

"I hope you saved me a dance."

It was then that she realized that the quiver of feeling on her neck had been Brandon's lips. Felicia turned.

"Brandon."

He smiled, the moon revealing his even white teeth.

"Are you having a good time?" he asked.

"Yes, of course," Felicia said, frustrated by the defensive note she heard in her own voice.

"Are you going to dance with me?"

Felicia stared at him, frozen.

"The mayor is supposed to be bringing me—"

"Water. I know." Brandon smiled again. He nodded to a glass sitting on a table back near the chair Felicia had been resting in before she rose to walk along the veranda. "Dance with me," he said.

She wanted to say no. She should say no. There was no reason on earth why she should dance with Brandon Donnelly.

He slid his arm around her waist and pulled her against him. His heart resonated with steady beats that she could feel through his white tuxedo shirt. He drew her tightly against him, moving with a sultry rhythm to the slow song that drifted out onto the veranda.

Against her better judgment, caution forgotten, Felicia danced with Brandon, taking languid, sliding steps that barely moved them at all. The length of his long legs pressed against hers, his hips swaying in time with her own.

Desire, a long-forgotten pulsation of inner need, uncoiled, flashing like molten lava through Felicia's veins. She didn't even notice when her steps stilled. Brandon's arm tightened around her back while his other hand reached up to touch her chin.

"You're beautiful," he whispered.

Felicia stared hungrily into his eyes, wanting to believe in the tenderness that weaved through his words. His blue depths were shadowed by the night.

Brandon met her gaze head on, searching her face for some sign of emotion that would mirror the physical response he sensed in her body. He restrained the urge to pick her up and carry her home, where he could ravish her all night long.

If he was going to prove that she'd never stopped loving him, he would have to be patient.

But there were some pleasures he couldn't wait to sample. He leaned closer, his heartbeat quickening. Felicia smelled sweet, fresh, and very feminine. She tried to pull back at the last minute, as if she'd grown suddenly afraid, but he wouldn't let her.

With one long finger, he lifted her chin and settled his mouth over hers with a sudden and irresistible demand. He plundered her mouth, gently prodding apart her lips until she welcomed him in. Her body relaxed against him, and he savored the warm taste of her tongue, swirling and exploring against his own.

He withdrew from her lips and wandered across her cheek, kissing her ear, partaking of the silken softness of her lobe, then moving down to the long, creamy column of her neck. He discovered the hollow at the base of her neck and traced its boundaries with his tongue before sliding his tingling touch up her throat to her chin. A soft moaning cry escaped her lips, sending torrents of hot need flashing through his body.

He didn't want to stop. But he had to. Eight years of unsatisfied longing for Felicia were going to explode if he didn't put an end to the wildness that her caresses invoked.

Brandon drew away from her lips, his breath coming fast and sharp in his chest. She met his eyes with a shaken, confused darkness. He detected vulnerability in her gaze.

He'd gone too far. The last thing he wanted to do was scare her with the power of his reaction to her kisses. He struggled inwardly to steady his breathing, to balance his emotions.

Felicia was so beautiful, so womanly. Through the protective shield she wore, Brandon sensed the uncertainty, the fear. Hard-edged on the outside, her soul bloomed like a rare, hidden orchid that only he had found.

He yearned to take her face in his hands and kiss her again, kiss her until they were both senseless with need and longing. Until she confessed she wanted him.

He cleared his throat and swallowed. He couldn't do that. If he did, he'd frighten her. She wasn't ready yet. It was too soon.

With one long, slow finger, he stroked a line down her smooth cheek, stopping to rub the fullness of her lower lip, swollen gently from his lovemaking. He lowered his hand to his side again, employing a strength he hadn't known he possessed before that moment.

"Welcome home," he said, his voice barely above a whisper.

"Felicia!"

They both turned sharply, the illusion of privacy shattered. Lola's tall figure stood silhouetted in the doorway that opened out onto the veranda from the ballroom.

"I've been looking everywhere for you, dear," Lola boomed as she hurried toward Felicia. "We'd like to get a photo with you and the entire Opera board to commemorate the ball. I've got everyone together."

Felicia's eyes flicked up to Brandon's. He thought he saw relief there. Relief and something else he couldn't identify.

Lola took Felicia's arm and pulled her along enthusiastically.

"You too, Brandon," Lola called over her shoulder.

Brandon sighed. Part of him was relieved, too. Relieved that matters had been taken out of his hands before he changed his mind and grabbed Felicia against him. Before he made love to her right there on the country club veranda.

But another side of him, the part of him that burned with liquid fire at the memory of Felicia's soft scent and satiny skin, wished Lola had never found them.

He watched as Lola and Felicia disappeared inside the ballroom. After a moment, he followed, bending to pick up Felicia's glass of ice water on the way in. Brandon downed the drink in a single gulp, vainly attempting to douse the fire within.

Felicia let Lola drag her away, lost in the confusion of Brandon's lovemaking. The laughter and chatter of the ballroom hit her like a blast of reality. In the warmth of the crowded room she felt the flush of his touch sweep away.

How could she have let him kiss her that way? she thought. And she'd kissed him back, returned caress for intoxicating caress. She'd been seduced by the crisp, fresh evening air, the moon overhead, the lovers kissing in the gazebo. Not to mention the two glasses of bubbling pink champagne she'd had at dinner.

Brandon had made her want him. She'd responded—oh, how she'd responded! Heat raced to her cheeks as she recalled the way she'd betrayed her desire with the fervent maneuvering of her tongue. And how he'd persuaded her, delighting her every sense with his enrapturing and sensual exploration.

She shut her eyes tight, embarrassed by the memory of her arousal at his kisses. He'd known she was moved by his lovemaking. He'd forced her to reveal her desire.

And she'd made it so easy for him. She'd fallen for his embrace without a second's hesitation.

But she wouldn't let it happen again, she determined, fighting back the wave of emotion that settled thickly in her throat. He wouldn't find her so easy the next time.

SIX

Felicia woke to a loud clanging from the kitchen. She rolled over with an irritable groan and peered at her digital clock. Six-fifteen, the glowing green numbers read. Her aching head reminded her that it had been past midnight before she'd gotten home from the Opera House Ball, and two hours after that before she'd been able to sleep.

She heard Robin's laughter, followed by her high-pitched, excited chatter. A deeper rumble came next, and she knew that that must be Brandon. Felicia lay quietly and listened. Not that she could understand the exact words from her distance, but she perceived instead the rhythm of joviality and anticipation. A part of her longed to join them, but she curled up quietly on her side instead and waited for them to leave.

Within moments, the clatter softened and stillness came over the house. Felicia rose and slid back the bedroom curtain a few inches. Outside it was dark except for the red and green lights from Brandon's boat, swaying in its slip. His tall form, illuminated in the beam of the lantern in his hand, towered over tiny Robin as he helped her into the fishing boat. Libby was already seated in the vessel.

Felicia tamped down an irrational swell of envy as she watched the trio. Brandon stepped down into the boat, looking up toward the house as he did. Felicia flicked the curtain back in place, retreating from her position by the window.

You're being ridiculous, she told herself harshly.

She took a shower, trying to convince herself she enjoyed being home alone, that she didn't want to be with them.

After all, she didn't care about fishing. Messy, smelly way to spend time, she'd always thought. She remembered Jake Donnelly as an avid fisherman. If he wasn't actually out on the lake fishing, he was canoeing out to check his trotlines in the cove, or simply standing on the shore casting lures into the water. At the very least, he'd have a fishing rod propped securely on the dock while he mowed or clipped hedges, so he wouldn't risk missing "the big one," as he'd liked to joke. He'd instilled his joy of fishing in Brandon. It was a true measure of Felicia's feelings for Brandon that she'd gone fishing with him several times during that fateful summer. She hadn't ever gotten used to it, though, or truly enjoyed it. She had just wanted to be with Brandon.

And wasn't that why she wished she were out on that boat right now? she thought suddenly.

She shook her head, desperately casting away the fog of the past that persisted in locking itself around her thoughts. After donning a pink T-shirt and blue shorts, she emerged to find the chaos Libby had left in the kitchen. Libby had prepared pancakes for Brandon and Robin, to impress the former rather than the latter, Felicia was sure. A half-empty pot of lukewarm coffee rested on the stovetop.

Felicia poured the pot out, recalling suddenly the first morning after she'd arrived back in Granbury. Brandon had rushed to his house to bring her a jar of instant, determinedly insisting on making her a cup of coffee. She smiled at the memory.

In so many ways he was the man she remembered from her past—joking, teasing, and funny. Yet in so many other ways he wasn't that man. The man she'd known eight years ago wouldn't have pushed her into a position that could harm her career.

As she automatically set about making a fresh pot of coffee and clearing up the clutter of dirty dishes, her thoughts wandered to the night before. She'd been angry with Brandon for persisting in his desire to drive her to the country club.

But she'd gone with him. She didn't have to. Sure, he'd made annoying suggestions about how it would look if she hadn't driven with him, but she could have brought Libby and Robin with her to ward off his attention.

She could have, if she'd wanted to. But she hadn't.

Then he'd made those insulting remarks about her career. Fluff roles!

Felicia poured a cup of hot, fragrant coffee and sipped gingerly as she considered his words the night before in his car on the way to the fundraising ball.

Afraid. He'd accused her of being afraid.

She took a larger gulp of the fresh brew than she meant to and burned the tip of her tongue. She grimaced.

Preferring to avoid emotion, in work and in her personal life, was sensible, she told herself defensively. It just meant she had more common sense than most people. Why set yourself up for pain?

She'd had plenty of pain dumped on her without her consent—the abandonment by her father before she was even born, followed by the desertion of her mother when she was five, and eventually the death of her grandmother. Not to mention the lack of security or sense of belonging that had always plagued her.

Felicia hadn't asked for any of those emotional struggles. They'd simply been unloaded on her, most of them when she was extremely young. She'd discovered at the age of five that even those people you expected to love you the most would inevitably leave you.

Her father was a faceless name she'd never met. The last she'd heard of her mother was a postcard on her eleventh birthday. She'd wondered if they'd show up after she became well-known. But they hadn't.

Her grandmother had loved her, but she'd always known she wouldn't be there for her forever. Her grandmother had been in fragile health even when Felicia was five. She'd warned the young Felicia that she had to learn to care for herself because she wouldn't be there for her when Felicia grew up.

There were only two people besides her grandmother that Felicia had ever given herself permission to open her heart to. Robin was one. And the other one was Brandon.

She'd loved him until she'd frightened herself with the power of her emotional need for him. Giving herself, body and soul, to Brandon had been intoxicating, beautiful, and overwhelming. That last summer had been like a joyous fantasy. Felicia had felt a freedom of spirit that she'd never experienced before.

Then he'd told her that he loved her and asked her to marry him. Her heart wanted to say yes, but she felt sick inside at the thought. If she married Brandon, she would have to give up her chance to go to Hollywood. She was afraid of staying in Granbury, of depending on someone else. Of depending on Brandon. Her grandmother had instilled in Felicia the need for self-sufficiency and success too deeply for it to be easily put aside.

Felicia's mother had given up college to run off with a smooth-talking ex-con. He'd left her pregnant and alone, her reputation damaged, her chance for an education set aside.

No, giving up career goals for a man was a mistake. Felicia had learned that lesson well.

Laying her heart open by admitting she loved Brandon and agreeing to marry him would only have set her up for pain. The sweet words of love he'd spoken should have made her happy, but they'd scared her instead.

She had known that she couldn't stay in Granbury, bear his children, and wait for the day when he would inevitably leave her. She had forced herself to focus on what was important—career, self-sufficiency. Self-protection.

She'd left his proposal unanswered when she packed her bag, kissed her grandmother goodbye, and drove west. She had determined to be successful on her own and to guard her heart. And to forget Brandon and the sort of pain that could come with that type of emotion.

Then last night on the veranda of the country club, Brandon had kissed her, taken her mouth and her heart into his. Nothing had changed. He was still capable of consuming her senses. In his presence, she couldn't trust herself. She wasn't in control, secure in the orderly existence she maintained for herself.

Brandon had swept her away, frightening her with the emotional response he inspired. And he had known it. She'd seen it in his eyes. He'd raked her soul with his blue eyes, uncovering her secret vulnerabilities.

Setting her coffee cup carefully on the counter, Felicia raised one slender finger to her mouth, reliving the sensation of possession his lips had demanded.

He'd used her physical response to his erotic assault to break through the barriers she'd always maintained between herself and others. He'd made her show that she wanted him and that she hadn't forgotten the passion they'd built together.

But just like the benefit show, the kiss could be another way to hurt her for the way she'd walked out on him. There wasn't a future for the two of them. When the benefit show was over, they'd go their separate ways. Maybe they'd never see each other again.

And that thought hurt, she confessed to herself, pressing her eyelids together as if to block the bruise to her heart. Brandon was one of the few people in her life she'd allowed herself, for a brief time, to love. And he was one of the few people who could hurt her.

Even after all these years.

Stupid, she chastised herself. It was stupid to let her feelings go on a rampage like this. He shouldn't be able to hurt her. Not now. Not after all this time. Not after she'd walked away from him exactly so she could avoid this kind of emotional conflict.

Felicia shook her head, clearing back her thoughts. There was no need for any of this, she told herself sternly. She and Brandon didn't have a relationship. Everything they'd ever had was in the past. Their kisses the night before had been a mistake, the product of a romantic atmosphere, a full moon, and a little too much champagne.

Even Brandon probably realized by now that it had been a mistake, she thought. When he'd driven her home at midnight, he'd been quiet, reflective. He'd said little in the car and had merely squeezed her hand as he told her good-night at the door of her grandmother's house.

It had been his way of telling her that the kiss had meant nothing, Felicia decided. She doubted he'd had trouble sleeping after he got home, or that he was spending the morning reliving every aspect of those stolen moments on the country club veranda.

No, Brandon was carefree as a lark. He was out on the lake soaking up the fawning attention of both Libby and Robin. If he was worrying about anything, it was probably that she might have taken their kiss more seriously than he'd intended.

She'd set him straight on that in no uncertain terms, Felicia resolved.

"I'm bored."

Brandon turned a frosty gaze on Libby. She'd been complaining about being bored since thirty minutes after they'd motored away from his dock.

"I'm having fun," Robin piped in from the end of the boat. She cast a brilliant smile at Brandon.

"That's because you caught a fish," Libby sulked. "I haven't caught anything, and I'm bored."

Brandon glanced at his watch with a bleary eye. They'd been on the lake for three hours. So far, he'd pulled out four stripers. Robin had reeled in a yellow catfish so large he'd almost lost it when he helped her draw in her line.

"Don't take us back yet," Robin begged, leaning over to touch Brandon's arm.

He smiled at the little girl. She reminded him so keenly of Felicia as a child. Robin's face held the same fresh innocence of Felicia, but without the wounded, retreating edge.

"Okay, another hour, then that's it," he told Robin. Libby's loud sigh spoke of her displeasure.

Robin beamed, and a trickle of unexpected joy filled Brandon as he smiled back at her through his tiredness. He wished he could see Felicia this happy. Easy and carefree, without the hesitancy, the distance she created whenever anyone tried to come close to her.

Memories of the night before had bounced around his brain all morning. He'd been unable to sleep for hours after he'd come home from the Opera House Ball, thinking of Felicia. After Lola had interrupted them on the veranda, Felicia had regrouped, becoming even more distant than before.

On their way home in the car, Brandon hadn't known what to say to her to break through her reserve. What could he have said that wouldn't have scared her? If he had come right out and told her he was falling in love with her all over again, she would have run.

He'd confessed deep feelings to her once before, and she'd disappeared from his life for eight years. This time, he had to take it slow, make her want him without frightening her.

When he'd walked her to her door after the ball, he'd done no more than squeeze her hand. The smoldering fire they'd built on the country club veranda had been barely under control. He hadn't trusted himself to kiss her again, not when it was dark and they were all alone, away from the crowd at the ball. Away from anything or anyone to stop them if they fanned the flames they'd sparked between them earlier.

He wanted to show her he could restrain himself, that he wouldn't push her. She needed time, and he was prepared to give it.

But he wasn't going to stop wooing her. She would be his. That was the only thing about which he had no doubt.

"Bob Combs here."

Felicia flipped shut the slim local phone book and shoved it across the kitchen counter. She'd spoken so rarely over the years to the realtor who managed the rental on her grandmother's house that it had taken her several moments simply to remember his name.

"Hi. This is Felicia Marick." She hesitated. "You've been handling the rental on my house here in Granbury."

"Oh, yes, Ms. Marick. I hope you found everything in order when you arrived?" Bob Combs said, his deep, even voice ending on a qucstioning note.

"Yes, it's fine."

"Great luck that the tenants moved out last month," Bob Combs added. "You called me just in time. I had a line on a young couple who were interested in signing a year's lease. They may still be interested. When you know when the house will be vacant again, I'll give them a call."

Felicia bit her lower lip. She'd made the decision, she berated herself. Don't stop now.

"No, don't do that," she said, then continued in a rush. "I've decided to sell the house. I want you to start listing it right away."

As soon as she hung up, the phone rang.

"Felicia! I just got back from the mountains and found all these messages from you," came the raspy voice of Noreen, Felicia's agent.

"I need to talk to you."

"Why? Is it about the movie?" Noreen asked, zeroing in right away on the matter of supreme interest to her at the moment.

Felicia's silence on the other end of the line answered the question.

"What? What's happening? Did you hear something?" Noreen demanded eagerly. "Has somebody else's name been publicized for—"

"No, nothing like that," Felicia broke in. She hated to tell Noreen what was happening with the benefit show. The agent hadn't wanted Felicia to come to Granbury in the first place. She could hear an "I told you so" coming, but Noreen had to know. "It's about the benefit show at the Opera House."

"What about it?" Noreen's voice sounded suspicious.

"I'm not playing Angel. I'm doing Veronica." There. She'd said it. Flat out.

Total silence met her announcement. Then chaos.

"What? That can't be. Why are you doing that?" A flurry of questions flew through the phone line. Felicia was tempted to hold the phone away from her ear, but she remained resolutely listening.

"The director insists I play Veronica. I can't just walk off the show."

"Who's the director?"

"Brandon Donnelly."

Noreen repeated the name slowly, thoughtfully. "Brandon Donnelly," she said. "Theater, right? Okay. He was in *Storm of Falcons* off-Broadway last year, right?"

"Right." And by all reviews, he'd been fabulous, Felicia couldn't help remembering.

"So does he have rocks for brains or what?" Noreen cried. "What's he doing casting you as Veronica? Didn't you tell him about the film? Hasn't he seen your work?"

Felicia patiently explained everything that had transpired between herself and Brandon at the Opera House office on Friday, or at least the parts she wanted Noreen to know about.

"He's not going to change his mind. I've tried," Felicia finished up. "I can't walk off the show."

"And this will decimate your chances at getting Angel in the film," Noreen added. "This was supposed to look like you were preparing for the film." She hesitated. Felicia could almost hear the wheels spinning in her agent's brain. "Okay, Felicia," Noreen continued, her voice serious, "we tell everybody you want the part of Veronica in the film. I'll start putting the word into carefully selected ears right away."

"What?" It was Felicia's turn to sound aghast. Veronica in the film? Playing Veronica at the Opera House was bad enough without extending it to the film. "She's not the kind of character I play."

"We'll say you're changing your image, going on to more serious roles," Noreen said, her words clipped and decisive. "We have to turn this around to our advantage, Felicia. This film's going to be a hit. I want you in it."

"I don't want to play—"

"You need this film, Felicia. In fact, this could be the best thing that's happened to your career in several years," Noreen went on. "Changing your image isn't such a bad idea. In fact, it's a great way to attract Huberts' attention just now, while he's considering the casting. It'll make you stand out from the pack when he's making his choices."

"But—"

"Well, I've got plenty of work to do now. I've got to run, Felicia. Call me if there's news. And don't worry about this deal. I'll handle it. You'll be in this film one way or another."

Noreen hung up. Felicia set the receiver back in its cradle and stared at the phone in disbelief.

It was nearly eleven o'clock when Brandon's boat rounded the tip of land where the lake opened into their small cove. Felicia lazed in the swing on the back porch, listening as the hum of the boat came nearer. She'd been fuming for several hours but hadn't gotten any closer to coming up with a solution to the upheaval Brandon's unwanted interference was causing in her life—both her professional life and her personal life.

He carefully guided his boat into his slip, and Libby and Robin climbed out, followed last by Brandon. Felicia waited on the porch quietly, watching Robin hurrying across the lawn, her short legs pumping as she ran.

"Mommy, Mommy," Robin called. "I got a fish!"

She giggled and huffed, nearly out of breath, as she skipped across the porch and tugged Felicia's arm.

"Come see," she entreated.

"Okay, okay, I'm coming," Felicia said, allowing her daughter to pull her from the porch and back across the yard to Brandon's dock. It was hard to maintain a cool demeanor when faced with an exuberant five-year-old.

They met Libby coming off the dock, tired, bedraggled, and wind-blown. Her red curls hung limp and damp around her face.

"No wonder you didn't want to go," Libby muttered as she passed Felicia. "I can't believe I got up at five and made pancakes so I could spend the most boring morning of my life surrounded by smelly bait and fish." She curled her lip in disgust. "He made me touch it."

Felicia wasn't sure if she meant the bait or the fish, or something else entirely, but figured she wouldn't ask. Libby turned and trailed away. Robin looked up at her mother with a twinkle in her eye.

"She didn't like it," Robin said.

"Apparently not," Felicia agreed.

She felt an irrational jolt of pleasure that Libby hadn't enjoyed her morning with Brandon. Then she reminded herself that not only was she angry with him for turning her career upside down, she had planned to tell him in no uncertain terms that he was to keep his hands—and his seductive lips—off of her in the future.

"I thought it was neat," Robin continued. "Look at my fish." She skipped over to Brandon, who was lugging a large, round yellow container up from the boat. About a half-dozen fish sloshed around in the water inside the plastic barrel.

"We're going to have a fish fry for lunch, Mommy," Robin said, tugging at her mother's hand. "Brandon's going to cook my fish. My fish is that one, the big one, see?" She pointed into the tub. "It's got whiskers like a cat." She laughed.

Felicia looked up and caught Brandon's gaze. He grinned down at her.

"My house or yours?" he inquired, a devilish flash in his blue eyes. His shirt hung stickily against his torso where he'd splashed himself while fishing. His smell was dank and watery, and just a little like fish.

And Felicia thought she'd never seen him sexier.

She frowned.

"Don't worry, I'm not going to make you clean the fish," Brandon said, grinning boyishly, seemingly unaware of the frustration simmering inside Felicia.

Robin jumped up and down beside her.

"We can have it at our house, can't we, Mommy?" she pleaded.

Felicia looked down into her daughter's round hazel eyes. There obviously weren't going to be any opportunities any time soon to have it out with Brandon. And she didn't want to argue with him in front of Robin. Upsetting her daughter was the last thing she wanted.

"Okay," Felicia agreed reluctantly. She flashed a warning glance at Brandon. He narrowed his eyes in response, a questioning light in the blue depths. She flipped around and walked off the dock, leaving Robin and Brandon to the onerous chore of cleaning the fish.

Brandon was good with Robin. She'd give him that.

Back inside the house, Felicia found the newly showered and dressed Libby drinking coffee in the kitchen and keeping up a constant flow of complaints on the morning's excursion.

"I got wet, and he didn't even care," Libby moaned. "He wouldn't go back. I was hot. He wouldn't bait my hook for me. . . ."

"Libby, you told him you loved to fish," Felicia put in, holding back the urge to laugh at Libby's self-indulgent griping. "What did you expect?"

Libby took a sip of her hot brew, then pursed her lips irritably.

"I expected it to be fun," she whined. "He was so boring. He kept telling me to be patient. And I was so uncomfortable and hot, and he kept telling me to be still." She stomped out of the kitchen. "I just hope he doesn't think I'm going to be the one cooking the stupid fish," she muttered on her way out.

Felicia poured another cup of coffee, smiling as she tipped the cup to her lips. Clearly, Brandon's shining image had grown a bit tarnished in Libby's eyes over the last few hours.

She could relate to that as well, Felicia reminded herself sternly. And she certainly didn't care if Brandon and Libby became involved. It was simply a matter of passing interest.

She walked into the den and glanced out the long windows overlooking the lake. Robin and Brandon sat on his dock, legs swinging out over the water. They had apparently put off cleaning the fish for the time being and were simply basking in the warm, fresh morning.

Felicia wondered again why he hadn't married after she'd left. After all, he'd been only twenty-two at the time. Plenty of time still to find someone else. He was thirty now. Why hadn't he ever wed? Surely not because he'd pined for her.

Fat chance, she scoffed to herself.

The fish, fried fresh and crispy in seasoned cornmeal, was devoured, the kitchen scrubbed, and Robin tucked in for a nap to make up for her early morning. Libby had declared herself due for some shut-eye as well and disappeared, so Felicia found herself alone with Brandon. She walked outside wordlessly, knowing he would follow her. She was determined not to talk to him in the house, where they might be overheard.

The last thing she needed was for Libby to find out she'd been kissing Brandon! She would never hear the end of it.

Felicia strolled to the shore and sat down on the seawall in the shade of an overhanging oak limb, dangling her legs over the side casually. By the time Brandon sauntered up and slung himself down beside her, she was prepared to greet him with an aloof nod that would have chilled a polar bear.

He tossed her a blasé smile as he settled in next to her. He'd taken a shower before lunch, and the fishy odor was gone, replaced by the spicy male scent that she remembered from last night. His fresh white T-shirt contrasted brightly against his dark, tanned skin. But it was his smile, framed by light laugh lines, that drew her eyes.

She forced herself to look away with a frown.

"Why don't you make yourself comfortable?" she invited sarcastically.

She couldn't allow herself to be drawn in by his enticing eyes, she warned herself. The decision she'd made long ago to depend on herself, not men, and certainly not Brandon, was the right one, she reasserted internally. She had to make him understand that she didn't appreciate his kisses or his interference in her career.

"I'm comfortable, thank you," he said, leaning back. His thighs, bare in his slim-fitting jean shorts, grazed the skin of her own legs, sparking a magnetic reaction that threatened to befuddle her thinking.

Felicia inched away. She needed to tell him what was on her mind, that she wanted him to leave her alone, get out of her life. The words stuck in her throat.

"Felicia?" His voice came soft and gentle beside her. She didn't look at him, staring out over the water instead. The clean, clear water of Lake Granbury sparkled like melted gold in the streaming rays of the afternoon sun. A light breeze had come up after lunch, giving rise to sporadic ribbons of white caps over the top of the water. "Felicia?" he spoke her name again.

He picked up her hand and stroked his fingers over

her skin. Her green eyes flicked up to his then, captured by the tenderness of his touch.

"I put the house up for sale." She hadn't meant to start there, but the words had rushed out anyway.

"You're selling your grandmother's house? Why?" he asked. The furrow between his brows told of his confusion. "You've kept the house all these years. Why sell it now?"

"It's time."

Brandon's frown deepened. He enclosed Felicia's hand between both of his own, drawing her attention forcibly to him.

"Why didn't you sell the house before now?" he demanded.

"I was renting it out. I—"

"You didn't need the money. Why didn't you sell it after your grandmother died?" he persisted.

Felicia stared at him speechlessly. Why hadn't she sold it? she asked herself. She pulled her hand away from his grip.

"You couldn't let it go," he answered for her. "You knew you'd come back here someday."

"I wasn't ever going to come back here," Felicia argued. "If it hadn't been for the Opera board, I wouldn't be here now."

"You came back here to save the Opera House?"

"Of course." Felicia stared at him. Then her eyes widened with knowledge. "You don't think I came back here to see you?" She laughed, a cold, hard sound even to her own ears. "I didn't know you'd be here."

Brandon smiled in a strained way.

"Right. You didn't think the Opera board would ask me to come back for the benefit show, too? Don't kid yourself."

"I'm not the one who's kidding myself," Felicia

countered. "You're the one with delusions if you think my returning to help reopen the Opera House has anything to do with you."

A moment of cool silence followed, broken only by the chirping of birds and rustling of leaves. Felicia turned to stare at the cove again, watching a fish fly up and dive down again, leaving a spiraling trail on the surface of the lake.

Brandon stared at Felicia's profile. Even in the shade, her skin glowed with golden good health. But in her eyes, he detected a lonely sadness. Her refusal to admit that her return to Granbury had anything to do with him didn't surprise him, but her barely suppressed anger did. Something was bothering her. Something more than his suggestion that she had hoped to see him in Granbury.

"What's wrong, Felicia?" he asked, forcing gentleness into his tone.

"Nothing."

He reached up and turned her face to his with a delicate finger across her cheek. He saw the distress in her expression.

"Tell me," he whispered.

Felicia looked down, then out to the lake again.

"I talked to my agent today," she said at last, her voice low.

"And?"

"She's going to try to get me the role of Veronica in the movie, instead of Angel."

Brandon could hear the frustration welling up in the thickness of her voice as she spoke.

"She's going to say I'm changing my image," Felicia continued, then she swiveled to meet Brandon's concerned gaze. "I hope you're pleased with yourself. Before casting me as Veronica in the benefit show, I had a good chance of landing Angel in the film. Now . . ." She shrugged, her words trailing off.

"Now you have a good chance of landing Veronica," Brandon finished for her. "And your agent's right. A change of image will be great for you. You're an incredible actress, Felicia. You can do it."

Felicia shook her head.

"You don't get it, do you, Brandon?" she returned heatedly. "I don't want to play that kind of role. It's not what I want."

"Why not?"

She hesitated.

"I'm not comfortable with it," she admitted finally.

Brandon met the pain in her eyes. He longed to lean forward and kiss her eyelids, kiss away the pain inside her.

"You can do it," he repeated. He reached out to squeeze her hand, but she drew away from him.

"Stop cheerleading." Felicia frowned. "I don't need it. You're the one behind all of this. You lured me to Granbury through the guise of the Opera board, let me think I'd have my pick of parts in the benefit show."

"None of this was aimed at hurting you," he said. "I don't want to hurt you."

"How do I know that?" she asked, confusion woven through her words. "How do I know you're not just angry about . . . about—"

Brandon placed his forefinger over her lips, stopping her from continuing.

"I'm not angry with you, Felicia. What do I have to do to prove to you that I don't want to hurt you for leaving me eight years ago?" he asked softly.

Felicia blinked but didn't turn from him. Brandon sensed the tumult raging inside her chest.

"You can stay out of my professional life from now

on,'' she told him, her voice shaky and low. She swallowed tightly. ''And you can keep out of my personal life, too. No more kisses and touches and . . .'' She stood up, brushing the grass from her shorts. ''Just back off!''

SEVEN

Back off.

Brandon recalled Felicia's final words to him as he leaned against the metal back of his folding chair, watching her reading lines from the script of *Passion's Pride* in her soft, sweet voice. Somehow he'd managed to hurt her, despite his good intentions.

Now she'd completely distanced herself from him. All morning she'd behaved coolly and professionally, repeating her lines, working dutifully on her role as Veronica. She'd listened without expression when Brandon had inserted his opinions on how a certain line should be interpreted, never arguing with him.

Her coldness concerned him. And he had no idea what to do about it. Trying to get close to her only sent her scurrying farther away. He'd obviously gone too far, too fast, already.

Wavy blond tendrils escaped the casual French braid hanging down her back, caressing her tanned cheek. Lowering his eyes, Brandon noticed the gentle swell of her breasts above the low, square-cut line of her yellow sundress. He wanted to throw down his script, jump off his folding chair, and hold her until she told him why she was avoiding him.

It was obvious she had some feelings for him. She desired him. Those kisses on the country club veranda hadn't been imagined. And he hadn't been the only one doing the kissing.

Felicia looked up then, her misty green eyes meeting his. She stared at him, no emotion showing in her face, then calmly turned her attention back to the script in her hand.

Brandon heard a movement behind him and turned, seeing the *Granbury Globe* editor, Wilbur Barron, making his way down the side aisle of the theater toward them.

"How's it going, Wilbur?" Brandon greeted the editor warmly, forcing himself to sound more jovial than he felt.

"Fine, fine," Wilbur answered. He tapped the reporter's pad he held in one hand with a ball-point pen. "Just got through looking at the contact sheets of my photos from the Opera House Ball. Got a couple great shots of you two that I'm planning on putting on the front page of Wednesday's paper. I'd like to have a full feature on you two to go with it, if you've got the time this morning to talk to me." He raised his brows hopefully at Brandon, then glanced at Felicia.

"Sure," Brandon agreed. He nodded to Felicia. "Let's go to my office." He turned to the rest of the group. "Let's take a short break."

Brandon led the way around to his office, followed by Wilbur and a clearly reluctant Felicia. She sat down quietly in one of the lumpy orange chairs in his office, waiting as if an executioner's ax were about to fall. Brandon was surprised to see how ill at ease she seemed to be with the press. Then he recalled the bitter tabloid reports he'd seen about her divorce from Rodney Kent, and he guessed she'd become gun-shy.

He waved Wilbur to another seat and settled in behind his cluttered desk. He handed Wilbur a program for *Passion's Pride*.

"Wilbur's been great about the Opera House reopening," Brandon said, turning to Felicia, hoping to relax her about the interview. "The local newspaper coverage has been excellent. Always very positive."

"Thank you so much," Wilbur said, grinning. "Wait until you two see the old photos we dug up from some of your performances at the Opera House eight years ago."

Brandon looked at Felicia. Her eyes flew up to his with an unreadable expression.

"Great," Brandon said, holding her gaze. "I'm looking forward to seeing them."

"Now, let's get down to business," Wilbur said. He plowed through a series of questions, checking background facts about both Brandon and Felicia's careers. Then he looked up at Felicia, his hand stilling over his pad. "You haven't been back to Granbury since you left the Opera House eight years ago, correct?"

"That's right," Felicia said.

"But you still own a house here?"

"It's for sale, actually."

Wilbur scribbled quickly.

"So you're not planning to return to Granbury again after this performance?" he questioned.

"No," Felicia confirmed in a low voice.

"You're not going to be making any future guest appearances at the Opera House, then?" Wilbur prodded.

She shook her head.

"We'll work on that," Brandon put in. He grinned devilishly across his desk at Felicia. "You never know what the future will hold."

She frowned and shot him a warning glare, fire lighting in her emerald depths. Brandon smiled broader. The fiery glimmer in her eyes warmed him. If it took a little mischievous provocation to shake her from her frozen silence, then that was fine by him.

Watching her act as if she'd died inside, like she had all morning, was unbearable for him. Especially since it seemed he'd contributed to her hurt.

"I don't have any plans to come back," Felicia told Wilbur. "That's why I'm selling my grandmother's house."

Wilbur looked up at her again.

"Why did you return for this show?" Wilbur asked.

"I wanted to help the Opera House," Felicia told him. "I got started here. This theater is a great asset to the community and needs to be reopened."

"What does the Opera House mean to you? What are some of your favorite memories?" the editor continued.

Felicia hesitated. Images flitted through her mind of Brandon ardently exploring every curve and dip of her body after their Opera House performances while they lay spread on a quilt under the glow of the Georgia moon. Brandon peppering her neck, her breasts, the softness of her inner thighs, with sensuous kisses burned in her memory. And she had returned touch for tantalizing touch, loving him with every beat of her heart.

Across the desk, Brandon was staring at her, waiting, his expression insufferably smug. As if he could read her mind.

"I can't remember anything in particular," Felicia said at last.

"You two used to be quite a hot item in those days," Wilbur prompted.

"Not really," Felicia said quickly.

"We sure were," Brandon said at the same time. He grinned cockily at her when she cast him a narrowed glare.

"You grew up together, next door to each other, right?" the editor asked.

"That's right. Felicia was like my kid sister," Brandon said. She rolled her eyes. "I taught her everything I know."

This time his gaze rested warm and suggestive on her, sending a heated pink flush to her cheeks. Somehow she guessed he wasn't talking about theater.

"I've learned a lot since then," Felicia said haughtily.

"But you never forget your first . . . acting partner," Brandon added.

"Time blurs everything," she said coolly.

Wilbur moved his gaze from Brandon to Felicia, then back again.

"Am I missing something?" Wilbur asked innocently.

Felicia smiled.

"Not at all," she told him.

Wilbur turned to Brandon.

"Lola Dunbar seems to believe you'll be staying on as the permanent managing director here? Is that so?"

Brandon shook his head.

"I haven't made any definite decisions," he told the editor.

Wilbur asked several more questions concerning the Opera House reopening, then rose. He stuck out his arm to Brandon, and they shook hands vigorously.

After shaking hands with Felicia, Wilbur thanked the two and made his way outside. Felicia moved to the door of the office and shut it firmly before whirling on Brandon.

"What are you up to now?" she demanded.

"I don't know what you mean," he replied mildly. He sat back down in his chair and propped his feet nonchalantly on his desk.

"You do, too, know what I mean," Felicia accused him hotly. "You know exactly what you were doing."

"And what was that?"

Felicia drew her lips together in a tight line. Brandon could be so impossible, she thought in irritation.

"You were making suggestive comments," she said, her tone carefully cool.

"Suggestive? Suggestive of what?"

Felicia crossed her arms over her chest in a protective gesture. Brandon noticed the way the pressure of her forearms against her chest pushed her cleavage together. He smiled.

"Don't laugh at me," she said with frustration.

"I'm not laughing at you, I promise," he assured her. He didn't think it would make her any happier if he told her he'd been enjoying her cleavage, so he let the matter slide. "Now, what exactly is it you think I was suggesting?"

Felicia sighed loudly. She said something in a muffled voice.

"What did you say?" Brandon asked.

Her eyes bored into his.

"Sex!" she repeated loudly.

"Sex," he said slowly, as if savoring the word on his tongue.

"Look, I'm only bringing this up because you seem to have the mistaken notion that you have some right to continue making these kinds of suggestive remarks,'' she said testily. ''Just because we were once . . . because we used to be . . .''

'' 'Lovers,' Felicia,'' Brandon finished for her, his lips lifting in a grin beyond his control.

She shrugged.

''Whatever. It's way in the past. And I'd appreciate it if you'd keep it there from now on,'' she said.

''And if you stop bringing it up, I will,'' he added agreeably.

Felicia pursed her pink lips together, then whipped around without another word. She slammed the door of his office, rattling the framed pictures on the office wall.

Brandon laughed, his heart lightening. She cared about him after all, he thought to himself, smiling.

Felicia watched Robin and Libby hungrily devouring their sandwiches and chips at the Top Crust Eatery and Bakery down the street from the Opera House, and her mind wandered to Brandon. She toyed with her fork, pushing around the lettuce and tomatoes on her plate, remembering the naughty gleam in Brandon's eyes when he'd said ''lovers'' to her.

He'd made the word feel like a caress. An erotic stroke.

She'd told him to back off. And she'd meant it.

Pushing aside the niggle of doubt that accompanied that thought, she stared out at the busy square. Shoppers and sightseers casually strolled along the sidewalk in the heat of the summer day, enjoying the pleasures of the historic town square.

''Can we come have lunch with you every day, Mommy?'' Robin asked. She picked up another chip and crunched into it as she waited expectantly for her mother's response.

Felicia smiled at the little girl.

"I don't think we'll do it every day," she told her. She glanced at Libby. "We'll see."

"How's your first day?" Libby asked.

Felicia feigned a smile.

"Okay," she said. "How about some apple pie?" she asked, changing the subject.

Libby and Robin nodded eagerly. Felicia stood up and walked to the counter to order three slices of fresh apple pie with ice cream. She heard the door of the eatery open and glanced around. Dory and another young actor from the company entered.

After Felicia placed the order and returned to the table, she was surprised to see Dory and the young actor approach.

"Hi," Dory said. She'd been friendly to Felicia all morning, the same as she'd been at The Tea Room days before. She smiled at Robin, then looked at Felicia questioningly. "Is this your daughter?"

"Yes, this is Robin," Felicia told her. "And this is Libby Hamilton."

"I'm five," Robin chimed in. She grinned. "We're getting pie."

"That sounds wonderful," Dory said. "I have a daughter the same age as Robin." She looked at Felicia. "Do you think we could sit with you? This is Ted Jarvis. You remember him from earlier?"

Felicia hesitated, then nodded. She didn't feel particularly in a socializing mood, but since there was still plenty of space at their table, she could hardly refuse. Dory and Ted drew up chairs from the next table and sat. The waitress brought their pie, and Dory and Ted ordered slices for themselves as well.

"I didn't know you were married," Felicia prompted, curious that Dory had a daughter.

Dory laughed, a soft, lilting sound.

"I'm not anymore," she said. "I'm divorced. Right after Cara was born," she explained. "It just didn't work out. I should have known. We were impossibly different." She shook her head, her straight brown hair cascading back and forth. "But I don't want to bore you with my problems." She grinned amicably.

Then she launched instead into a discussion about her daughter and the good and bad points of moving back in with her parents.

"It's just until I can get on my feet again," she said. "With the Opera House reopening, I hope things will get better."

"I'm glad," Felicia said, noticing suddenly that Libby hadn't stopped smiling at Ted since he'd sat down. They'd carried on their own separate conversation while Felicia and Dory had been talking.

"This is Ted's first job as a regular member of a company," Libby told Felicia, glancing at her briefly before returning her attention to Ted.

"Congratulations," Felicia said warmly. She watched Libby sipping her lemonade and gazing at Ted. Apparently, Felicia thought, Brandon had been replaced in Libby's affections.

"Do you know about the Summer Story Hour?" Dory asked Felicia.

"No. What's that?"

"It's a story hour at the library for the kids," Dory told her. "Either Mom or Dad takes Cara every Wednesday morning. Libby could take Robin. I bet she and Cara could be friends. Cara's kind of lonely, spending all her time with my parents."

"Oh, Mommy, could I?" Robin asked, her eyes wide. "Would she play with me?" she asked Dory.

"Yes, I'm sure she would," Dory said, smiling.

Felicia looked at Libby.

"Sure," Libby agreed. But her eyes remained on Ted.

"Goody!" Robin exclaimed. "How many days is it till Wednesday?"

"Two days," Felicia said.

Robin beamed.

"I can't wait," she said, then crammed a large bite of pie into her small mouth.

Felicia stood back, leaning slightly, staring at the newly tamed rosebushes that were set back against the side wall of her grandmother's house. Remembering Mrs. Parks's questions about her grandmother's prize roses, Felicia had determined to trim the neglected shrubs.

She found herself hoping that whoever bought the house would care for the roses like her grandmother had. Obviously, the rosebushes had been tended only sporadically by the various tenants over the years.

"Beautiful."

Felicia spun around at the deep voice, softly accented with a Southern drawl.

"The roses, I mean," Brandon said. The sunset sky warmed his face with brilliant gold rays. "You have your grandmother's touch."

Felicia laughed.

"I wouldn't say that," she denied.

"I think your grandmother would have been very proud of you," Brandon said.

Felicia met his eyes.

"I don't know," she said, looking down at the hedge

clippers in her hand. "I think Grandmother would have a few things to say about my life if she were here."

Brandon laughed.

"She was good at dispensing advice," he agreed. Then he held up a rolled newspaper in his hand. "I didn't know if you'd seen this yet." He unfurled the paper to the front page. The Wednesday edition of the twice-weekly local paper led with a piece on the Opera House Ball. A four-column grainy photograph of Brandon and Felicia standing at the podium at the country club, smiling as the crowd applauded, beamed up off the page.

"The best photos are inside," Brandon told Felicia. He opened the paper to an inside page. An old photograph from their summer eight years ago at the Opera House jumped out at Felicia. The photo showed Brandon and Felicia onstage, kissing. Felicia was struck first by how young Brandon looked. Then the meaning of the photo dawned on her, and she remembered when it had been taken. She remembered the performance clearly. It had been the last performance of that production. It was the night Brandon had asked her to marry him. The night she'd disappeared from his life.

Her eyes flew up to Brandon's. He waited, as if expecting some reaction from her.

Felicia swallowed uncomfortably.

"Thanks for showing it to me," she said, turning away to intently examine the rosebushes again. She reached out and clipped off a fragrant rose, lifting the sweet-smelling flower to her nose to inhale the scent.

"Do you remember the night this picture was taken?" Brandon asked. He was so close she could feel his breath against her ear.

"No," she lied without turning.

"I do."

Felicia pivoted slowly. Brandon stood close, his fresh, male aroma mingling with the sweetness of the red rose in her hand.

"I don't," she insisted. A weak, rubbery feeling shuddered up her legs. As always when he was near, she sensed his magnetic draw. His sexual aura.

"It was the night I asked you to marry me." He stepped toward her, narrowing the small gap between them to nothing. "You smell wonderful," he said, his eyes pulling hers into the blue depths of his soul.

"That's the roses," she whispered, struggling to maintain her composure.

"It's you," he said. He reached up and brushed back a lock of her corn-gold hair, pushing it behind her neck. "And before, when I said I meant the roses were beautiful, I lied," he continued in a husky, low voice. "I meant you."

"Brandon . . ."

His face flashed toward hers, and he covered her lips with his own, pressing inside with his tongue. Felicia started to push back with one hand, the other hand tightly gripping the rose. Brandon released her. Suddenly.

"I'm sorry," he said.

He turned around and strode back across the lawn, slamming his back door behind him as he went inside. Felicia stared after him. A twinge of pain finally brought her eyes down to her hand. A thorn on the stem of the rose had pricked her finger. She lifted her finger to her mouth and pressed the tiny wound against her tongue.

Brandon's kiss seared her memory. She closed her eyes, trying to shut out the feel of his lips against hers.

She failed.

* * *

"I don't know. I'm exhausted." Felicia shook her head tiredly, trying to smile gently at her young daughter as she did.

The week of rehearsals had been draining. From reading through the play line by line, they'd quickly progressed to full rehearsal. With only two weeks to prepare a first-rate performance, there wasn't any time to spare. The nights at the theater had become later every day, and by Saturday, Felicia felt completely enervated.

More tiring than the long hours had been plunging heart and soul into the character of Veronica. But Felicia had determined not to fail at her performance in the benefit. She had no choice but to put her all into the show. Her entire future hinged on her ability to carry off the difficult, emotion-packed role. With each rehearsal, she found herself less and less able to retain the emotional detachment she'd so long maintained.

She'd actually cried after one particularly long, dramatic stretch of dialogue between her character and Brandon's. When Brandon had hesitated and reached out to her, Felicia had turned away quickly. A quick toss of water on her face in the bathroom and she'd returned, ignoring his questioning glances, vigilantly keeping her distance.

The hurt of Veronica as she releases Stefan to Angel struck close to home. Too close to home. But Felicia had no choice but to continue. Her future rode on the outcome.

On Saturday, Brandon promised to let everyone go home earlier than usual to get in some much-needed rest before beginning another arduous week of rehearsals. Libby and Robin had popped into the theater at eight, hoping to lure Ted and Felicia to a late dinner at nearby Peppermint's.

Libby and Ted stood to the side of the stage, hands linked, eyes twinkling into each other's. Robin stared up at her mother with an imploring expression. Most of the company had already dispersed their separate ways for the evening.

"Please, Mommy. Ted said they have banjo players at Peppermint's on Saturday nights," Robin begged. "I've never heard a banjo, Mommy. And I could have ice cream, too."

Felicia laughed. She suspected the ice cream had a lot more to do with Robin's urge to go to Peppermint's than the banjo players.

"Okay," Felicia agreed with a sigh. She hadn't spent much time with Robin lately. It wouldn't take long just to have a quick meal at the sandwich shop across the square.

She took Robin's small hand into her own and emerged onto the square outside the Opera House, followed by Libby and Ted. The evening light was falling gently over the old town square. Traffic moved sporadically along Main Street, humming softly in the night air. The four of them walked leisurely down the sidewalk, then crossed to Macon Street and on down to Peppermint's. Light and music drifted outward from the sandwich and ice cream shop.

Peppermint's was close to being full to capacity. The four of them grabbed the last table against the side wall and, after a quick perusal of the menu underneath the glass-topped table, ordered sandwiches, chips, and sodas all around.

While they awaited their food, Felicia leaned back to enjoy the pleasant country music emanating from the band of locals in the Players Parlor at the back of the restaurant. For as long as anyone could remember, an assortment of various-aged musicians had been gathering at the sandwich shop and ice cream parlor every Saturday to offer freely of their talents to the shop's patrons. Whoever showed up played and sang whatever they and the crowd wanted.

Tonight, Felicia could pick out a good eight or nine musicians banding together on the makeshift stage, exuberantly playing their banjos, fiddles, and guitars. A piano player accompanied the group from a piano set up against the side wall.

The mellow mix of country-western and folk music soothed Felicia's tired nerves. Her lashes drooped down, and she drifted softly with the lilting melody.

"Mommy?"

Felicia's lashes flew up.

"Don't fall asleep," Robin cried over the music. "Look, our food's here."

Felicia inhaled deeply, rousing herself. She looked down at the plate in front of her, then smiled at her daughter.

"I'm awake, sweetie."

The sight of the appetizing sandwich revived her hunger, and she ate with as much delight as the others, stopping only to sip her soda and watch the musicians in the back. When they finished and the dishes were cleared, Ted leaned back and draped his arm casually around the back of Libby's chair. Felicia watched with a grin as Libby snuggled up against Ted.

"Can I get an ice cream cone now, Mommy?" Robin asked.

Felicia nodded and dug some money out of her purse. Robin skipped around the tables to the ice cream counter.

Scooting her chair around, Felicia positioned herself

with a view of the musicians. An enthusiastic rendition of the old country song "Hey, Good-Lookin' " filled the shop. Felicia closed her eyes again, letting the beat of the music thrum through her body, relaxing her.

The harsh scrape of a chair rubbing against the floor behind her opened her eyes. She turned to see Brandon pulling up a seat from the table behind them just as the singer belted out, " 'How about cookin' somethin' up with me?' "

Brandon winked at Felicia mischievously.

"Fancy meeting you here," he said in her ear, smiling.

"Fancy that," she returned, a sarcastic edge to her voice.

"You don't mind if I sit here, do you?" he asked.

"It's a free country," she said. She swiveled around, pointedly giving him her back.

But the mood was broken. The music no longer relaxed her. Her nerves vibrated, and exhaustion rippled through her.

Robin plopped back down at the table, two scoops of rich chocolate ice cream teetering from atop her sugar cone. She grinned a welcome at Brandon before starting to work on her treat. Felicia watched her child enjoying the simple pleasure, trying to push Brandon's presence from her mind.

Her daughter resembled her closely, Felicia knew. Robin's curly blond locks and finely drawn features came straight from her mother, as if Rodney's genes had played no part in her makeup at all. At five, Robin was the exact age Felicia had been when she'd moved to Granbury. The age Felicia had been when her mother had abandoned her.

It was eerie, Felicia suddenly thought, that she hadn't

brought Robin to Granbury until she was five. As if repeating some pattern from the past.

But, of course, she thought quickly, she would never leave Robin. Not like her mother had left her.

Felicia didn't want Robin to ever experience the pain she had when she'd been her daughter's age. Sensations of deeply felt loss, abandonment, and insecurity haunted her childhood memories, interweaving pain through the happier images of her grandmother's comforting arms.

She swallowed thickly, looking around suddenly at the high white walls, the whirling ceiling fans, the smell of freshly made sandwiches and cold ice cream.

And she gazed again at Robin. She remembered how she had sat right here, in this same sandwich shop, and eaten an ice cream cone while her mother explained that she would be leaving.

For so many years, she hadn't allowed herself to think about that day. She hadn't been able to recall her mother's exact words. Felicia's eyes glazed over as she stared at Robin. The little girl licked eagerly at her ice cream, turning it this way and that, catching with her tongue the soft drips that melted down the side of her cone.

I have to go, Felicia's mother had told her that day in the sandwich shop. *I don't belong here. I have to start fresh somewhere else. Nobody likes me here. They all talk about me, about how I ran off with your dad. They think they're better than me. Nobody loves me, and I can't love anybody. I can't give you the love you need. I can't love you and take care of you, not like your grandmother can.*

I have to go. I have to go. I can't love you. I can't love you.

The words rang over and over again inside Felicia's

mind. She squeezed her eyes shut, trying to block off the memory of the words, as she had for so many years. Until now, until she'd come back to this town, to this sandwich shop, with her own five-year-old daughter.

"Mommy, I'm finished with my ice cream. Are you ready to go?"

Felicia's eyes flashed up to her daughter. Robin stared back at her, chocolate rimming her lips.

"Are you ready to go, Mommy?" Robin repeated.

Tears rushed out all at once, and Felicia moved quickly, grabbing her napkin, vainly attempting to stem the flow of emotion from her eyes. Libby and Ted were staring at her now, their expressions confused.

"Felicia?" Brandon's voice came close and warm by her ear, tender with concern.

Embarrassment flooded through Felicia. She'd broken down, suddenly and, to her companions, inexplicably. Felicia never cried. She detested women who cried. Now this was the second time in less than a week. She dabbed at her wet cheeks, but tears swept down again.

"Mommy, are you okay?" Robin's voice raised with distress.

"Yes, sweetheart, I'm okay. It's just . . ." Felicia forced a watery smile across the table, pressing her napkin against her face again.

"Come on. I'm getting you out of here," Brandon said suddenly, tugging Felicia up by her arm. He gestured to Robin to stay with Libby. Too drained to protest, Felicia allowed him to pull her out the door of the restaurant.

Outside on the sidewalk, the cool evening air breezing over them, Brandon stopped, drawing Felicia's face up to his.

"What's wrong, Felicia?" His voice was soft but demanding.

Felicia stared up at him mutely. And started to cry again.

EIGHT

What had he done? Brandon wondered. Felicia had been fine when he'd walked into Peppermint's. He'd been looking for a quick meal and had found Felicia instead. He'd spotted her immediately, sitting casually against the wall enjoying the music, her long blond hair waving down around her shoulders.

But within a short time, he'd apparently reduced her to tears. Guilt flooded through him.

"Felicia, I'm sorry," Brandon told her softly, wrapping his arms around her, shielding her from the stares of passersby on the sidewalk in front of Peppermint's.

"I'm okay. Really," she said between sniffles. "I can't believe I did that. I'm sorry."

How right she felt in his arms, Brandon thought. She felt soft and womanly, a smooth, easy fit against his chest. He wished that somehow he could make whatever troubled her disappear. That he could kiss the pain from her eyes and bring happiness to her heart.

Felicia pulled away slightly to dab at her eyes with her hands, but the flow of tears down her cheeks remained unchecked.

"Let me take you home," Brandon suggested.

Felicia hesitated, bit her lip, then acquiesced.

"Okay," she said shakily. "I guess I'm not really fit to go back in there right now. But Robin—"

"Libby and Ted will take care of Robin," Brandon told her. "Come on."

He kept one arm around her as they walked across the square to his car. The drive home was short and quiet. Felicia stared out the window, saying little. Brandon decided not to push her. Not yet. But he was determined to know what was wrong.

Pulling into his driveway, he parked and turned off the motor.

"Felicia?"

She turned to face him, her expression shadowed in the darkness of evening.

"Thanks for driving me home," she said softly. She turned and got out of the car, slamming the door shut. Brandon rose, too, and reached out to grab her arm when she tried to walk across the lawn to her grandmother's house.

"Wait."

Felicia stopped and turned toward him.

"Don't go home," Brandon said.

"It's late."

"Felicia, we have to talk."

"I'm tired."

She turned from him again, tugging her arm from his grip.

"Felicia, damn it. No!" The frustrated anger behind the words came as a surprise even to Brandon.

Felicia stopped short and stared up at him, her eyes wide and dark.

"Brandon—"

"You're going to talk to me whether you like it or

not,'' he said, his teeth gritted tightly together, his cheeks set in hard lines.

''I don't want—''

''Playing this your way hasn't gotten us anywhere,'' Brandon ground out, seizing her elbow firmly with one hand and guiding her up to the front door of his house. ''We're doing this my way now.''

Felicia was silent while he turned the key in the lock and pulled her inside. He didn't let go of her arm until they'd reached his den, where he led her to the long, plump blue couch against the side wall. Wide windows to the lake mirrored their reflections against the darkness outside.

Brandon sat down beside Felicia, his heart pumping wildly. He hated forcing her into his house this way, but he wasn't going to let her get away. Not again. She was talking to him whether she wanted to or not.

He looked into her face, and what he saw there crushed his fury. Tears pooled in her emerald eyes, shining with raw hurt.

Brandon leaned forward, pressing one hand over his forehead. He closed his eyes, trying to block out the pain he'd witnessed. The pain he'd caused.

''I'm sorry, Felicia,'' he said in a near whisper.

Silence, deep and long, followed. Then he felt a touch, a gentle, hesitant stroke, against his shoulder. He opened his eyes and looked at Felicia.

She stared back at him, her misty green eyes rimmed with redness. Need reflected back at him from her darkened depths. Her lower lip quivered. Brandon moved toward her and she slid into his arms without protest.

Laying her soft blond head against his shoulder, she cried. Brandon held her, motionless at first, then he rocked gently, smoothing his hand over her tumbling curls.

"I'm sorry. I'm so sorry," she whispered, her voice thick with emotion.

Brandon drew back enough to touch his fingers to her cheeks, to tenderly trace the path of a tear. She gazed up at him, vulnerable and open.

"Why are you sorry?" he asked her, caressing her cheek, then her chin, before moving a lock of hair behind her shoulder.

"I can't believe I broke down like this," Felicia told him. "I don't do this. I'm so sorry. You must think—I don't know what you think. I'm sorry."

"Stop apologizing." Brandon shook his head firmly. "You've been through a great deal since you came back to Granbury. And I've been responsible for a lot of it. I'm the one who should be apologizing to you."

Felicia squeezed her eyes shut, then opened them to study Brandon intently. She licked her lips and shook her head. She started to speak, but tears sprang to her eyes again.

"Felicia?"

She shook her head.

"I'm okay," she insisted. "It's just . . . it's just . . ."

"What?" he demanded. "What's wrong?"

She blinked, tears falling slowly down her cheeks.

"You don't have anything to be sorry for. I know you didn't mean to hurt me," she said at last.

Brandon felt as if his heart nearly stopped beating altogether.

"You mean you believe I didn't try to sabotage your career?" he asked. He could hardly believe his ears.

"Yes," she whispered.

He gazed into her still-moist eyes.

"Why has that been so hard for you to believe?" He waited, as if for an eternity, before she answered.

"I don't know," she said, staring down at her lap.

"I guess believing you wanted to hurt me was easier than believing the alternative."

"And what is the alternative?"

Felicia slowly raised her eyes to his, then looked back down before answering.

"What?" Brandon asked, unable to understand her muffled response.

"That you might really care about me," she said, louder this time.

Brandon's eyes widened. She found it hard to believe that he cared about her?

He reached out and tugged her chin to face him. Her eyes, dark and hungry, tore at his soul.

"Felicia, when haven't I cared about you?" he asked her softly. "I've never stopped caring about you. I've never stopped thinking about you. Not in all these years."

"I left you. I married Rodney, for all the wrong reasons. You have to hate me."

"I don't hate you."

He longed to tell her he loved her. But fear wrapped tight around his throat. He'd told her that once before, and she'd disappeared. She was so vulnerable now. He couldn't frighten her away.

"Why not?" she asked.

He smiled at her softly and smoothed his fingers along the line of her jaw.

"I could never hate you, Felicia," he said in a low, husky voice. "I tried, I admit it. I wanted to hate you." He hesitated, seeing the pain flicker in her eyes. He leaned forward and kissed her lightly on the lips. "But I couldn't. And I couldn't forget you, either. You've always been with me."

He sighed and leaned back, grasping her hand tightly

in his own, determined not to let her go. He turned to watch her as he spoke.

"I left Granbury, trying to escape the memory of you." He shook his head. "But you came with me to New York. In my heart and in my dreams. I never forgot you. Sometimes, I thought I had. But then I'd see you somewhere, in a movie or in a magazine. And you'd be back again."

He drew her hand to his mouth and pressed a gentle kiss on the back of her hand, then turned her hand over to rub the soft skin of her palm against his mouth. Her expression as she watched him was unreadable, but she didn't resist his touch.

"I had to see you again," he said. "And so when the Opera board called me . . ." He let the explanation trail off. Felicia was so quiet. Had he scared her? Had he said too much?

"Brandon."

He waited, studying her face as she appeared to struggle for words.

"You never forgot about me?" Felicia's heart felt so full, crowded with long-repressed yearnings and emotions that threatened to spin her out of control. Brandon's sweetness ripped at her defenses. She longed for nothing more than to throw herself into the safety of his arms. If, in fact, there could be such a thing as safety in someone's arms, she thought.

His eyes glowed with warm lights, soothing her with his kindness. Entreating her to believe in the power of . . .

Love?

The mere idea sent a ripple of discomfort through her. Her heart ached with memories of the past, of the short time when she'd given in to love with Brandon.

But the twinge of fear that followed along with that

memory reminded her to be cautious. She started to draw her hand from his, but he kissed her palm again. A shiver of longing for the past rolled over her.

"No, I never forgot you," he assured her. "How could I?"

He hadn't forgotten her. She wanted to believe he meant it. Her heart absorbed his words thirstily.

"Tell me why you were crying at Peppermint's," Brandon requested suddenly, his voice soft with concern. "Was it me? Was it because I was there?"

"Oh, no, Brandon," she told him quickly.

"Then what?"

How could she explain? she wondered. The hurt was too deep to share. She didn't know how to share it. She hadn't ever tried.

"I can't explain," she said.

"Try."

Felicia stared out at the dark windows.

"Brandon, I don't know . . ."

He sighed.

"I'm going to get us some coffee, Felicia," he said softly. He squeezed her hand before releasing it. "And then we're going to talk." The look he gave her as he spoke was both stern and gentle.

Felicia watched his tall, broad form move into the kitchen. She got up and followed him, leaning over the bar to study his back as he walked back and forth in the large country-style kitchen.

He quickly put on a small pot of decaffeinated coffee in the automatic drip machine, then found two flower-patterned cups and saucers in the cupboard. Holding up one cup, he smiled at Felicia.

"My mother left this set of dishes here," he explained ruefully. "Not exactly my taste."

Felicia tilted her head to the side.

"I think they're lovely," she said softly.

Brandon walked to her, leaned forward over the counter, and touched his hand to the side of her face. The warm light of the kitchen cast a golden shimmer over his chestnut hair. He smiled.

"You're the lovely one," he said.

Felicia looked down, and Brandon removed his hand.

"Do I make you uncomfortable when I tell you how beautiful you are?" he asked.

Felicia grimaced.

"Maybe a little," she admitted. "But don't stop."

He leaned back his head and laughed, and she joined in, her mood lightening momentarily. When the coffee was ready, he poured two cups and carried them into the den.

They sipped their coffee and talked about his parents, a subject about which Felicia could chat easily. But she knew he hadn't forgotten his earlier question.

She toyed with her coffee as long as possible, but she set the cup down empty at last. Brandon set his down as well and reached for her hand, intertwining his fingers with her own. Then he drew her toward him, pulling her against his side. She allowed him to, enjoying the warmth of his touch too much to resist.

"Felicia?" Her name came soft and low by her ear.

He waited, and she knew what he was waiting for. She knew, too, that he wasn't likely to give up.

Brandon had known her since she was five, but she'd never discussed her mother with him. She'd never talked about her mother at all, not even to her grandmother. Her grandmother had usually acted as if Felicia's mother was dead.

And as for Brandon, he came from a happy, close-knit family. He could never understand her pain.

"Talk to me, Felicia. I want to know why you were crying at Peppermint's. Tell me what I did."

"It wasn't you, Brandon," Felicia insisted. She stared up into his eyes, meeting the concern there.

"Then what was it?" he asked

She took a deep breath and exhaled slowly.

"I was just remembering," she said in a low voice.

"Remembering what?"

A short silence filled the room.

"My mother," she said finally. Then she told him. She told him how she remembered, as she was watching Robin eat her ice cream, about the day her mother had taken her to the same restaurant when she also was five. That had been the day her mother had left her, she explained.

"I guess I'd blocked out what she said to me that day," Felicia said quietly. "It came back to me all of a sudden when I was looking at Robin."

"What did you remember her saying to you?" Brandon asked gently. He pulled her closer, wrapping her in his warmth.

"She said . . ." Felicia stopped, emotion choking her throat. Then the words tumbled out. "She said she had to leave me because she didn't belong here. She said nobody loved her, and that she couldn't love me. Then she left me."

Brandon was completely still for a long moment. *He doesn't understand,* Felicia thought quickly.

"Felicia." Brandon turned toward her, drawing her around to face him. "You've had this locked up inside of you since you were five?" His eyes were dark, and she could see the angry lights in them. "No one should treat a child that way, say those things to a child."

Then he pulled her against his chest and held her tight. Felicia heard his heartbeat, fast and strong.

"I knew your mother had left you with your grandmother, but I didn't know it had happened like that," he said to her, bending back to see her face. "Your mother must have had a lot of problems of her own, Felicia. You were too young to handle the things she said to you."

"I never told anyone," Felicia said softly. "My grandmother and I never talked about my mother. I learned to push away thoughts of her so I wouldn't have to deal with the pain. I blocked out the words she said that day."

"Maybe from your memory, but not from your heart," Brandon said.

He was right, Felicia knew. The fact that he saw right through her, saw how the pain had shaped her life, surprised her.

"You've always seemed afraid to let anyone in." He said it as a statement, not a question. "You were burned so badly as a child that you don't want anything to do with love. I think you don't want anyone close enough to you to hurt you."

His finger trailed a slow, delicate path along her jawline as he spoke. His eyes captured hers and wouldn't let go.

"That's why you left me, isn't it?" he asked, his voice a mere whisper.

Felicia didn't answer, and Brandon tugged her to him again. He knew he couldn't push her into any further confessions tonight. She'd opened her soul to him more already than she ever had before. He'd give her time.

Felicia leaned against him, her physical and emotional exhaustion obvious. Brandon stroked her hair, watching the way the blond tendrils caught the low light from the lamp, sparkling with fiery glimmers.

"You're tired," he said.

She murmured in agreement. Brandon snuggled her closer, offering the warmth of his embrace. Felicia felt so small and vulnerable in his arms. He believed he could hold her forever.

Her hair smelled sweet, like the roses in her grandmother's yard. He wanted to press his face into her thick hair, smother her neck with gentle kisses, love away her pain.

He loved her more deeply than ever, he thought with an awed sense of wonder as he stared down at her head. Maybe he'd never even stopped loving her.

He moved his hand in slow, rhythmic strokes down her cheek to her shoulder, then along the curve of her waist. He touched her only softly. No matter what his body craved, he'd do no more than hold her tonight.

Her regular, even breathing led him to think she slept. His back grew stiff, but he remained still, not wanting to disturb her.

"Brandon?"

He pressed his hand against the soft curve of her waist.

"I need to let Libby know where I am."

"I'll call her," Brandon assured her, "in a little while."

A companionable silence stretched between them.

"Brandon?"

He waited quietly.

"I never forgot you, either," she whispered.

She turned around and settled deeper into the crook of his shoulder, snuggling against him. It was the last thing she said before she fell asleep.

Felicia relaxed on a quilt as she leaned against the broad trunk of an old shade tree, watching Robin wriggling excitedly from her position across the park.

Granbury's Fourth of July celebration was in full swing, and Robin had drafted Brandon as her partner in the three-legged race.

"Go Robin!" Felicia called as the race began.

Halfway down the course, Robin stumbled. Then Brandon tripped over her, and the two of them lurched together onto the grass. Brandon came up laughing, Robin squealing, and together they rose in clumsy determination and dragged along to the finish line.

Felicia leaned back against the tree trunk, laughing. Robin came running across the park, pulling Brandon along behind her.

"Bravo! Bravo!" Felicia called, clapping.

"We lost," Robin announced, grinning.

"I noticed," Felicia agreed.

Brandon smiled boyishly at her, pushing back his damp hair from his forehead. The afternoon typified the usual sweltering, humid summer heat of Central Georgia.

A ripple of pleasure went through Felicia as she smiled back at him. She was taken aback anew at how handsome he was.

"I need some lemonade," he said. "Want some?"

Robin and Felicia nodded eagerly, and Robin plopped down beside her mother to rest while Brandon headed in the direction of a concession stand.

Felicia watched him weave carefully through the crowd and thought of how kind and considerate he'd been in the past week. Ever since the night she'd fallen asleep in his arms, after the incident at Peppermint's, Brandon had been close by her side. Not demanding. Just there.

It had annoyed her when she first came back to Granbury that Brandon seemed to show up everywhere she turned. Now his presence comforted her.

In rehearsals, he'd been watchful of her needs, helping her through the difficult scenes as she worked into the role. The last week had been easier somehow than the first. Playing Veronica didn't seem as painful as it had in the beginning. Felicia wasn't fighting it as much, resisting the emotion. She allowed herself to fall in with it, and a new satisfaction, a joy even, in the depth of the character was starting to fill her.

She even found herself looking forward to the first show. The debut of the production had been timed to coincide with the high tourist draw of Granbury's Fourth of July festivities. Brandon and Felicia rode at the head of the Fourth of July Parade as grand marshals, sitting in a long white convertible with a banner advertising the Opera House show. Robin rode with them and laughed and waved as they slowly drove around the town square. The sidewalks of the square were lined with beaming, welcoming faces who called out and applauded as their car moved by.

The happiness in her daughter's eyes reaffirmed to Felicia the rightness of her decision to relax her normal restriction against allowing Robin to appear with her in public. Riding in the parade was too big a treat to deny the little girl.

They'd decided to take a few hours after the parade to enjoy the celebration before Felicia and Brandon returned to the Opera House for last-minute rehearsals. A picnic in the park and the three-legged race sounded like heaven.

Anything sounded like heaven with Brandon, Felicia realized suddenly. She was falling for him. And she was letting herself.

Her mouth tugged gently upward at the corners as she observed him moving back toward her through the crowd. Between his hands, he balanced three plastic cups of lemonade.

"Too bad we didn't win," Robin said with a sigh. "I think Brandon's really neat. Don't you, Mommy?'

Felicia's lips settled into a full-fledged grin.

"Yes. He's neat all right," she agreed.

"You're incredible! They love you!" Brandon threw his arms around Felicia and drew her against his chest in a bear hug of congratulation. The play was a success. Felicia was a success. He knew it, and she knew it. The feeling, the emotion, the timing, it had all been there. The heady rush of performance glowed in her cheeks.

He'd never seen her more beautiful. Or more happy.

The curtain swept up for a second time, and Brandon took Felicia's hand and approached the audience. They bowed together again to the roar of the audience, now on its feet.

The small, century-old stone building was packed to capacity with more than three hundred attendees at the first show. Metal folding chairs had been set up in the side aisles to accommodate as many eager theater-goers as possible. The reopening of the Granbury Opera House was a resounding triumph.

Brandon released Felicia's hand and stepped back, leaving the stage to Felicia. She looked at him questioningly and he nodded. Moving forward, she bowed once more before stepping back to rejoin him.

The curtain brushed down for the final time, and Felicia and Brandon were quickly surrounded by their castmates. Amid much clapping on the back, hugging and compliments, Felicia and Brandon had to struggle to find each other again.

"Thank you!" she shouted to him.

He said nothing but covered her mouth with his, not caring who saw them. She kissed him back, her tongue darting erotically in her exhilaration, sending shooting spirals of desire through Brandon's bloodstream.

"Thank *you,*" he growled when the kiss ended. Felicia grinned at him.

Someone pressed champagne glasses into their hands, and they both drank deeply of the bubbly beverage, smiling into each other's eyes. The scene around them was boisterous and loud.

"Ride with me to the party," he shouted in her ear. "Meet me by the back door."

Felicia nodded and pushed her way back to the dressing room to prepare for the planned cast party at the Dunbars' house. Several female cast members in various stages of undress already crowded the room as Felicia hurriedly pulled off her stage clothes and scrubbed her face of the heavy makeup that was necessary under the bright lights. After applying a light layer of makeup and slipping into the peach sequined off-the-shoulder dress she'd brought with her for the party, she wove back through the crowd to the rear entrance of the Opera House.

She stepped into the freshness of the night air and immediately heard a low whistle. Turning, she smiled into Brandon's appreciative eyes. Her gaze raked his lean form, taking in the black slacks and white tuxedo jacket, then moving up to his smoothly handsome face.

"You look incredible," she said.

"I think it's against the law to look as good as you look," Brandon teased. "At least inside the city limits."

He slipped his arm around her waist, and Felicia felt the desire between them like a palpable force. She remembered all those long-ago nights when they'd performed at the Opera House together. She remembered what they used to do after the shows.

She knew he was thinking about it, too.

They talked about the show on the way to the Dunbars', but the looks that Brandon was sending her way made it difficult for Felicia to keep her mind on the Opera House. She was sorry for the drive to end when they pulled up in front of the Dunbars' house a few minutes later. The turn-of-the-century Victorian home, only a few blocks off the square, glowed with inviting lights. From its gingerbread trim to the state historical marker in the front yard, it epitomized the sense of place and roots that Felicia had looked to with longing as a child.

Now, as an adult, she was being welcomed into the Dunbars' home as an honored guest. But she realized ruefully that she'd rather be sharing this moment of triumph alone with Brandon.

Placing her hand in his, she reluctantly rose out of his car and joined others on the sidewalk crowding up to the Dunbars' front door. Inside, the house was packed with company players, Opera board members, town officials, and Opera House backers. The smells of wine, perfume, and cigarette smoke filtered through the rooms.

Brandon kept a close hand on Felicia's elbow as they moved slowly through the house, stopping to smile and talk to people as they went. Their course seemed aimless to Felicia. She didn't know why they were there, except that they were expected to be there. She didn't want to be there.

She stopped suddenly, in a corner, and stared up at Brandon.

"How'd you like to get out of here?" he suggested to her over the noise of the revelry.

"You're on," she responded eagerly. "I've got to find Libby and Robin first and let them know. They're supposed to be here somewhere."

They weaved around several people and moved through a doorway, running almost smack into Libby, Robin, and Ted. Dory's daughter, Cara, stood next to Robin.

"Mommy!" Robin cried, hugging her mother. Libby, Ted, and Cara smiled. "The show was so neat, Mommy. Everybody really liked you, didn't they?" Her eyes shone with pride.

"Thank you, sweetie," Felicia said.

"Cara's going to spend the night with us, if that's okay, Mommy," Robin said. "Her mother and Libby said it was okay if you said it was okay."

Felicia nodded. "Just don't give Libby a hard time, all right? Be good, and go to bed when she says." She looked at Libby. "We're going to go ahead and leave now. I'll be home later. Don't keep Robin here at the party too much longer."

"I won't. Don't worry," Libby told her, a curious sparkle in her eyes. "Ted's going to come back with us, too, so the girls will have plenty of supervision. Everything will be fine."

Felicia hugged Robin again, then laced her fingers through Brandon's as they made their way toward the front door. She was relieved that Libby hadn't asked her any questions. She was sure that Libby had guessed already that Felicia and Brandon were growing closer, but Felicia wasn't ready to talk about it yet. Their closeness was still too new, too fragile, to bear up under the analysis she knew Libby would put it under.

The last thing Felicia wanted to do was analyze what she was doing.

Within minutes, she and Brandon quietly escaped

into the crisp night. The sounds of celebration receded into the cool air as they clasped hands together like children playing hooky from school and ran to Brandon's car.

"Everyone will wonder why we left the party so early," Felicia said with a playful giggle.

"Let them," Brandon said carelessly. He smiled at her as he keyed the ignition.

Instead of turning toward home, he headed in the opposite direction. Felicia spoke of the play as he drove, her high-pitched, excited chatter warming his heart. He told her over again how wonderful her performance had been, how the crowd had loved her.

"It was you, Brandon," she argued. "I couldn't have done it without you. You were fabulous." She stopped and looked around suddenly. "Where are we—"

She broke off and her mouth dropped open.

"Brandon?"

Sliding the car to a smooth halt, he parked beneath a large live oak tree. Beyond lay a dark, quiet clearing nestled alongside the shore of Lake Granbury. A private, secret place they'd been to many times that summer eight years ago.

A place for lovers.

NINE

"You do remember this place?" Brandon asked her, his voice deep and tender in the stillness of the dark car.

Felicia stared into the inky depths of his eyes.

"Yes," she whispered.

Brandon smiled warmly and pushed open his car door. He came around the side of the car and gave Felicia his hand as she stood. She licked her lips dryly, as if uncertain of his intentions. Her eyes darted to his, and in the milky moonlight he saw vulnerability. And hope.

He slipped his arm around her back, not wanting to push her too far or too fast. Together they walked between the trees and across the thick springy grass to the lake's edge. Only a few miles from the heart of the square and down a forgotten lane off the highway, the clearing had lain unused and untouched for years. Evidence of aborted plans to build a home on the spot were seen in the electric and water lines that had been brought out to the property, signs of lost intentions that had been there even eight years ago. Nothing had changed. The stand of oak trees still separated it from the road and protected it on two sides, leaving the clearing open only to the lake.

It still made a perfect, sheltered place for lovers in the dark of night, under the cool of the Georgia sky. The water lapped gently against the marshy shore. The white glimmer of the moon splattered in a changeable pattern over the water.

Felicia moved her hand over Brandon's back, taking him closer to her side. He looked down at her, and she met his gaze openly.

"I have a lot of good memories of this place," she told him.

He nodded.

"Incredible memories," he added.

"I tried to forget this place," she said. "I tried to forget you."

Brandon turned toward her, his back to the lake. He placed his hands on her shoulders, leaning forward to place a kiss on the satiny smooth fullness of her lips.

"The past is behind us," he suggested, moving to nibble the delicate lobe of her ear. "Together, we can make more memories."

"Make memories?" Felicia questioned, bending back to study his face. She grinned. "Now what exactly does that entail?" she flirted.

His dark blue eyes glowed in the pale light. Felicia's happiness filled him with delight. And desire.

He'd wanted to see her happy for so long.

And he'd desired her even longer.

"Memories are like magic," Brandon told her in a sultry whisper full of sensual promise. "It's best to show rather than tell."

Felicia laughed, a soft, tinkling sound that echoed merrily in the quiet of the country night.

"I don't have my scrapbook with me," she teased.

"Lucky for you, I have mine," Brandon said.

He took her hand and led her back up the mild slope that rose from the bank of the lake. When they finally stood at the trunk of the car, Brandon reached into his pockets for his keys. Felicia watched him, brows furrowed with confusion, as he unlocked the trunk.

He bent into the shadowed space and lifted up the large patchwork quilt they'd used at the picnic.

"Your scrapbook?" Felicia inquired.

Brandon's lips turned upward at the corners.

"In a manner of speaking," he replied. "Remember, magic requires imagination." He lowered the trunk lid and slipped the keys back into his pocket, holding the quilt against his side. He linked the fingers of his free hand with hers, and they walked slowly back toward the water.

When they reached a smooth, even spot close to the lake, Brandon dropped the quilt and bent to spread it along the soft ground. Felicia stooped beside him and began helping to unfold the thick quilted blanket.

Her fingers accidentally touched his, and they both stopped to gaze up at each other.

"This is our quilt, isn't it?" she asked him.

She knew the answer without his telling her, but she wanted to hear the words. She wanted the dream that was wrapping around her heart to have the validation of his voice.

"Yes," he said.

"I didn't notice earlier, at the picnic. I didn't think—"

"Of course not," Brandon said, his words laced with amusement. He lifted one brow quirkily. "It was probably the first time you'd ever seen it in the light of day."

Felicia laughed again, and the sound of their merriment rolled out over the water. He was right, she thought happily. The long, passion-filled hours when the quilt had served them so well had always been at night, under the same Georgia sky that hung above them now. They'd lain on the downy quilt after shows at the Opera House, just like tonight, and made love. And memories.

"Your scrapbook, huh?" she prompted.

"I see a lot of memories here," he said. His expression turned serious suddenly. He took both of Felicia's hands into his own and pressed his fingers against her palms. "If you don't want to be here with me, like this, we'll fold this up right now. I don't want to push you too fast. I don't want to scare you."

His eyes held hers for a long moment, taking her into his soul with the intensity of his gaze. If she said no now, he would take her home. He'd sworn not to push her beyond what she was prepared to give.

Looking into the dark emerald pools of her eyes, he hoped with every fiber of his soul that she'd stay. The desire to show her he loved her throbbed through his being. The steady beat of her nearness pounded in his bloodstream.

"I want to stay," Felicia whispered.

A ripple of sheer ecstasy, a hint of joy to come, shuddered through him. With the gentlest of touches, his lips descended onto hers. He kissed her softly at first, only pressing his mouth against hers. Then her lips parted beneath his enticing assault, inviting him inward to enjoy the pleasuring wonders of her tongue.

He explored everywhere, running the tip of his tongue along her perfectly even teeth and the soft inner lining of her mouth. Then they joined in a delectable tango of tongues, reveling in the impassioned dance of discovery. The wildness of her movements delighted him. Felicia came to him eagerly, wantonly.

He loved the taste of her, leaving the sweetness of her mouth only to caress the slim column of her neck, discovering the enchantment of the hollow of her throat with his tongue. He kissed the curve of her jaw, then bent back with a moan as she moved to draw her tongue down his own throat.

She touched him with skillful provocation, lingering at the base of his neck to pepper him with amorous kisses that sent shivers of anticipation through his veins. Her hands undid his tie, then moved to the small buttons of his tuxedo shirt, unbuttoning them with swift flicks of her nimble fingers. She smoothed her hand over his bared chest, spreading her fingers through the light sprinkling of hair.

Brandon reached down, pushing her away long enough for him to pull off his jacket and shirt. Then, with a light caress, he reached behind her back and brought down the zipper of her peach dress. With a soft smile, Felicia stood and stepped out of the dress, revealing herself to him completely, aside from the brief wisps of underclothes she wore. She knelt back down before him.

With a sensation of both awe and heated need stirring through him, Brandon brought Felicia down against the patchwork quilt. Her face glowed with muted light from the moon overhead. She glowed with something else as well, he thought as he stared down at her. He saw love and hope and passion.

Felicia lay back against the old quilt without resistance. Her lacy white bra, designed for off-the-shoulder wear, shone bright, catching the glimmers of the night sky.

She started to unclasp it, but Brandon stopped her

with a flash of movement. Then, with a slow, tantalizing stroke, he drew his finger down the column of her neck, across her breastbone, to the cleft between her full breasts.

He cupped one rounded breast through the silky material of the bra, gazing up into Felicia's eyes as he did. Then, with his other hand, he quickly unhooked the front fastener of the garment and whisked it open. The band of white material fell back to the ground behind her.

The pearly whiteness of the untanned skin of her breasts reflected the filmy moonlight. Brandon, leaning down beside her, trailed his mouth over the rosy tip of first one breast, then the other. With looping, swirling motions, he encircled the bud of each breast in turn, pleasuring them until they tightened under the ardent onslaught.

Excitement waved through his body as he heard her soft sighs of rapture. Then she rolled over him, pushing him back against the quilt. She laved his neck and shoulders with her tongue, inspiring ripples of aching impatience.

But he wanted this to be slow, so slow. He wanted Felicia to be as fulfilled as he already knew he'd be. They'd waited eight years for this. He wouldn't hurry it.

She lay atop his chest, showering his neck and chest with soft sizzles from her tongue. Her breasts were bared against his flesh with an almost unbearably erotic pressure. Brandon dug his hands through the tangled tumble of wheat-blond curls that fell forward over her shoulders, struggling to restrain the passion building inside him.

Then Felicia turned to him again, her fingers burning down toward his navel. She bent to kiss the indentation there, transforming the small dip into a carnal hollow by sliding her tongue flirtatiously around its edges before moving southward.

Slipping her hand around the rim of his slacks, she pushed them down anxiously. Brandon accommodated her desire, raising on one arm to help her eliminate the restriction of his clothes. As he removed his slacks and briefs, his need for her was immediately evident.

Felicia touched him, smoothing her hand down his heated shaft. Circling with her thumb, she moved upward then down in a seductive stroke that shot spirals of longing pulsing inside Brandon's loins.

"I want you," he whispered to her, staring into her green eyes. She leaned down to brush his lips with her mouth, her fingers still partaking of their sensuous, rhythmic motions below.

He moved forward then, pressing her down to the quilt, halting her sweet seduction while he still had the strength. He easily slipped her lace and satin panties down her hips. With an enticing wriggle of her bottom, she slid them off.

His attention was drawn inexorably to the exposed softness of her womanhood. He touched her gently, then delicately probed the silken folds. She opened to him, spreading her slender legs apart in a gesture of invitation. He plunged his finger inside her, encouraged by the satisfied moan she delivered at his invasion.

Brandon pleasured her, stroking her heated inner flesh, kissing her stomach, her navel, her thighs, as he explored her femininity. Then he raised over her, meeting her nakedness with his. He turned his eyes up to hers again, a question in his gaze.

She smiled softly, and he entered her moist valley with a long, fast stroke. He moved at heartbeat pace, the beauty of the moment rolling over him in undulating waves of euphoria.

Felicia took him, deep and strong, loving the fullness of body and spirit, wishing it would never end. His eyes held hers, and she lost herself in his dark depths, feeling the joining that went beyond their physical movements.

Then suddenly, he pulled her over atop him, spinning her around so that he never left her. Now the plunging rise and fall of his manhood delved deeper, producing higher surges of passion. She felt both numbed and electrified at the same time. Shudders of ecstasy came out in cries of joy.

As Felicia straddled him, leaning in close to kiss him and gaze into his eyes, her long blond hair fell around them like a cloud. Her golden tresses created a secret cocoon, a hidden Eden all their own that no one could enter but them.

Her low sighs, her soft breaths, her sultry, sensual rotation above him, broke his restraint. Brandon could hold back no longer, and he gave vent to his need. With deep pulsations of energy, he surrendered to the desire they'd both built, then pulled Felicia down to hold her tightly against him.

They both breathed heavily for several moments, drained from the vigorous lovemaking. Felicia leaned her head back and smiled into Brandon's hooded eyes. She touched her finger softly along his cheekbone, then kissed his chin.

"Good scrapbook," she murmured, with a sexy, teasing twinkle in her eyes.

"Like it, do you?" He smiled back at her.

She nodded.

"You make great memories," she told him, bending to scatter kisses across his chest.

"You make great magic," he replied.

Then he used his hands to grip her by the waist and pull her up toward him so he could kiss her deeply on the lips, invading with his tongue, tasting of her sweetness again. The heaven they'd created was something he'd never experienced with anyone else, not in the eight years since they'd been apart.

"It's only magic with you, Felicia," Brandon whispered.

She stared down at him, her lips swollen from his kisses. Beyond them, the lake lapped softly at the shore as a light breeze ruffled the water. Above, the brilliant stars decked the night sky, shedding a dim glow over the earth.

"Magic," Felicia repeated the word slowly, relishing the feel of it on her tongue. The night was magical, she thought. It was as if time had reeled backward, and she and Brandon were young and innocent again. They'd come to this lakeside hideaway so many times in the past to make love and share private secrets and laughter.

Now here they were again, rediscovering their enchantment. Reliving their passion.

"Do you believe in magic?" he asked her, rubbing his hands down the delectable curve of her lower back. He felt ribbons of desire flaming inside him again, sparked by the sensual titillation of her bare breasts against his flesh.

Felicia's mouth tilted upward.

"Convince me," she said, brushing erotically over him, teasing him with the suggestive gyration of her hips.

Brandon growled hungrily and moved to prove his point.

* * *

Felicia woke to the soft touch of a finger brushing lightly across her cheek. She stretched sleepily, her eyes still shut. Brandon's face entered her thoughts, and she smiled. A warm, pleasurable sensation soaked through her from head to toe as she recalled their long hours of lovemaking. A particularly soothing tingle settled in somewhere around her middle.

Without thinking, she reached for him. Then she remembered she was in her grandmother's house, in bed, alone.

"Mommy?"

Felicia's eyes flashed open. Robin sat on the edge of her bed, one hand rubbing gently over her mother's cheek.

"I didn't think you were ever going to get up," Robin said. She made a small bounce on the bed. "You're not mad at me for waking you up, are you? I didn't ask Libby if I could. I was afraid she'd say no."

Yawning, Felicia nodded.

"It's okay, sweetie." She turned to look at her clock. Eight o'clock. She'd gotten only five hours of rest. Then she smiled again, thinking that Brandon's lovemaking at their secret place along the lake was the reason why.

That had been worth losing a little sleep for, she thought. More than worth it.

"Libby helped me and Cara make pancakes," Robin said brightly. "Will you come eat some?"

"Of course," Felicia agreed, realizing suddenly that she was ravenous.

Robin grinned, then leaned down to give her mother a quick hug.

"I like Cara," Robin said. "You know, she's the same age as me. Except she's two months older." She pursed her lips thoughtfully. "But she's going to be in kindergarten this year, too. If I was here, we could be in the same class."

"Well, maybe," Felicia said. "There are probably lots of kindergarten classes."

"But we might be," Robin persisted. A serious expression came over her face. "I wish I lived in Granbury all the time, like Cara."

Felicia stared at her daughter, an edge of worry creeping its way into the comforting remnants of last night's passion. The entire evening, from the exhilarating Opera House show to the final, reluctant kiss from Brandon's lips, had been like a dream, a fantasy. This morning was reality. And reality was that she and Robin didn't live in Granbury. They had a life in California, and they were going to return to it. Soon.

"We live in California, sweetie. You like it there. You have friends there." And now wasn't the time that Felicia really wanted to have to think about it. She wanted to dwell on last night, on Brandon's kisses. And a few other things.

"Not like Cara." Robin's mouth was set in a glum line. Hoping Robin would lose interest in the conversation, Felicia asked casually, "What about the kids in your play group at home?"

Robin pushed her lower lip forward.

"I don't like them. They don't even know how to fish. I bet they don't even know what a catfish looks like."

Felicia forced herself to laugh, trying to lighten the mood between them. Most of all, she wanted to push back the growing darkness inside her that was shadowing the glow left over from last night.

"Then you can tell them all about it," she told Robin brightly. "Remember all the things you like about California, like our house, your room, the beach, Disneyland.''

Robin rolled her eyes.

''I've been to Disneyland lots of times,'' she told her mother. ''I've never been to Six Flags Over Georgia. Not even once. Cara's been there, and she says it's really fun. And I like the lake better than the ocean. There aren't any sharks in it.''

Felicia watched her daughter silently. She could see Robin was serious about wanting to stay in Granbury. The idea of her daughter's being hurt when they left Granbury bothered her. It was a possibility that had never occurred to her before they had arrived.

A lot of things had never occurred to her before they had arrived. Like that she would see Brandon again.

Felicia sighed. Thinking about going back to California was the last thing she wanted to do this morning. She and Brandon had found each other again last night. They'd created a private enchantment all their own.

But the real world had broken in already, chipping away at the fantasy. And Felicia didn't want it to. She didn't want to think about harsh reality. Not yet.

''I don't want to go back to California,'' Robin said in a whiny voice.

''Hey,'' Felicia said, pretending cheer, ''we'll get frown lines if we worry. That's what Noreen says. I think you'd better show me those pancakes, okay? I'm starving.'' She smiled at Robin.

Felicia looked up at the sound of a light tap at the door. Libby peeked around into the room.

''I'm sorry, Felicia. I didn't know she was going to come back here and wake you up.'' Libby smiled apologetically. She was already showered and dressed in a neon-pink shorts and top outfit, and she wore dangling silver earrings. Felicia had a sneaking suspicion that Ted would be over.

"That's okay," Felicia said, shrugging. "Time to get up, anyway, right?"

Encouraged, Libby pushed the door open farther and came in.

"Go fix a plate for your mother," Libby told Robin. The little girl jumped up obediently and ran back down the hall.

"Were the girls good last night?" Felicia asked, raising up and plumping her pillow against the headboard before leaning back again.

"They were fine," Libby said impatiently. "I want to know about you."

Felicia shook her head.

"There's nothing to tell," she said. Then her mouth split open in a wide grin that she couldn't restrain.

"There is, too!" Libby cried. "Tell me." She sat down on the bed in the spot vacated by Robin.

"No!"

"Come on."

Felicia shook her head again, sobering.

"Look, there's really nothing to tell, Libby," she insisted. She swallowed tightly, a sudden rush of emotion choking her. What had happened between herself and Brandon last night was too private to share. And too delicate. Their new beginning felt fragile to Felicia, as if it might break apart if she spoke of it aloud.

In fact, she was afraid it was breaking apart already. The light of day alone might do the job.

"What's going on?" Libby asked, concern filling her voice. "You looked happy, but now you look like you're about to cry. What gives?"

Felicia sighed. How could she explain to Libby that she was afraid she was in love with Brandon? And as it had been eight years ago, their futures lay in separate directions.

Her conversation with Robin had reminded her all too keenly of what lay ahead. She and Robin were leaving Granbury when the show's three-week run ended.

She hadn't thought of that last night. Brandon's nearness had wiped everything from her mind. Simply recalling those hours by the lake sent shooting tingles through her body again, like tiny aftershocks of their desire.

"I know you were with Brandon." Libby raised her brows hopefully. "He's a really nice guy, Felicia."

"Yes, he's real nice," she agreed.

"Well," Libby said, rising off the bed, "I know something that'll cheer you up."

"And what's that?" Felicia asked, glad for a change of subject.

"Last night, after we got home, Howard Huberts called. Twice." Libby stared at her expectantly. "Well? Aren't you excited? He was at the show. He said he came to Georgia just to see you in the benefit, and that he had a plane out again last night. He wanted me to tell you congratulations on your performance. Isn't that great?"

A numbing sensation fingered over Felicia's heart. Howard Huberts, the director of the film version of *Passion's Pride*. He'd been at the Opera House.

It was proof that he actually was interested in Felicia for the role of Veronica in the film. And he'd called to offer his congratulations. Noreen would say that was a good sign. A very good sign.

If she landed the film, there wouldn't be any question at all about whether or not she was going back to California right away. She wouldn't have to make any hard decisions.

Without warning, the vision of Brandon's dark eyes, gazing into hers as he moved inside her, crept into her thoughts. She thought about leaving him. Again.

"Aren't you excited?" Libby prodded.

Felicia blinked several times, pushing back the moisture that threatened.

"Sure. That's wonderful," she said distractedly. And a small, proud part of her did think it was wonderful. She'd proven she could play a different sort of character than she ever had before. She'd impressed Howard Huberts.

Brandon had helped her do that.

Her heart swelled with love. And hurt. She couldn't stay. She couldn't go.

"You smell incredible."

Felicia bent her neck upward and looked straight into Brandon's cobalt-blue eyes, shining down at hers, his skin crinkling at the corners as he smiled. Her confusion melted away as if it didn't exist.

He pressed a soft kiss behind her ear and growled, a sound full of promise and seductive innuendo.

"I wish we hadn't had to go home to separate beds," he murmured. "I could have spent the whole night with you. I missed you."

Felicia grinned and glanced teasingly at the slim gold watch on her arm.

"We've only been apart for seven hours," she told him, motioning for him to grab one of the other lawn chairs and join her under the shady pecan in the yard. The lake glittered before them, fresh and still in the morning sun.

Brandon pulled up a folding chair beside her and

slung down into it, his long legs splayed out in front of him.

"Well, seven hours is far too long," he said easily, a sultry tone in his voice. He reached over and picked up her hand. "I want you to be the first to know, Felicia. This morning I told Lola I was accepting the job as permanent managing director of the Granbury Opera House."

Felicia wanted to congratulate him. The words stuck in her throat. She stared down at her feet, unable to meet Brandon's eyes any longer.

"Felicia? Is something wrong?"

She wore her blond locks loose today, tumbling wildly about her shoulders. She looked sexier than any woman had a right to, Brandon thought. And he wanted to press her down against the thick green grass and take her like he had last night, wiping away any hint of trouble from her soft eyes.

"Felicia?"

She looked up then.

"I'm leaving." Her voice was flat, hopeless-sounding.

"What?" Brandon furrowed his forehead. "We just finished the first show. We have three weeks to go."

"I don't mean now. I mean in three weeks."

Brandon twisted his lips together as he considered her words. She had a life in California, he knew. He didn't expect her to give up her film career.

But he was hoping she would modify her life. Maybe just a little. She could afford to keep homes in two places.

"Huberts called last night after the show. He told Libby to tell me congratulations. He was at the show." She stared at him, waiting.

"That's great," Brandon said.

Felicia sighed.

"Don't you see? We have to leave," she insisted.

"You'll come back." He shrugged as if the problem was solved.

Felicia shook her head.

"I live in California. My work is there, even if I don't get this film. And Robin's school will be there." She looked down again.

"Why does it have to be one or the other?" Brandon asked gently, rubbing the pad of his thumb in a swirling motion around her palm.

Felicia stared up at him, startled.

"I can't drag Robin back and forth," Felicia persisted.

"Doesn't Robin like Granbury?"

Felicia hesitated.

"It's not Robin, is it?" Brandon's voice came softly to her. He laced his fingers between hers. "And it isn't work, either." He raised her hand to his lips and pressed a tender kiss on her skin.

She didn't answer.

"You're afraid," he said. "You're afraid because you know that I love you." Felicia's eyes darted to his, captured. He felt her try to pull her hand away, and he held it tighter, refusing to release her. "And most of all, you're afraid because you're in love with me, too."

"Brandon—"

"I'm not going to push you," he assured her. "I want to give you time. But you have to give us time, too. You don't have to decide today that you're going back to California and that you're never going to see me again."

Felicia was silent a moment, as if considering his words. She allowed him to hold her gaze, her green eyes big and vulnerable.

"You're in love with me?" she whispered. His words stunned her. Her confusion and protests evaporated under the bewitching power of those wonderful, incredible words.

Frightening words. But Felicia pushed back the twinge of fear and doubt, wanting to believe him, craving the enchantment he offered.

Brandon laughed at her expression of wonder and, sitting up, he pulled her forward off her chair into his lap with one fast move that was too quick for her to resist.

"Of course, I do," he cried loudly, wrapping his arms about her soft curves. She felt incredibly right in his arms. "I love you, Felicia Marick!" he shouted, and surprised laughter burst out of her, falling around them like joyful raindrops.

She hadn't admitted she loved him, but he knew she wasn't ready for that. Happiness and warmth rushed through Brandon, and he squeezed her against him, pressing his lips to hers and kissing her fiercely. She answered with equal abandon.

He had three weeks to convince her that she loved him—and that she couldn't live without him.

TEN

"I always thought if I came back here, there'd be condos," Felicia said softly, lying on her stomach, leaning up with her chin resting against her balled fists. She stared out at the lake gleaming under the starlit sky.

"What?" Brandon asked, snuggling against her, throwing one arm casually over her backside. He trailed an exploratory finger down the curvature of her spine beneath her loose-fitting T-shirt.

"Condos." Felicia stared at him, her emerald eyes glowing darkly. "I thought somebody would have built condos here by now. Or tract houses. Or a hotel or something."

"They wouldn't dare," Brandon said. He leaned over to kiss her ear. "This is our place. If somebody tried to build here, they'd be struck dead. Or something."

Felicia chuckled. "That's comforting."

Brandon pressed his lips against her nose, her eyelids, running his fingers down the side of her cheek and through her golden hair. Then he rolled her back against the quilt with a soft stroke, inviting her to an encore of the lovemaking they'd just concluded.

"Some things never change, aren't meant to change," he whispered as he brushed behind her neck the hair that tumbled around her shoulders.

Felicia stilled. She'd tried to push her confusion about the future from her thoughts during the past weeks. And in the midst of performances, publicity appearances, and Brandon's frequent attention, she'd almost succeeded.

They'd just completed their second weekend of performances, with seven evening shows and matinees packed in between Thursdays and Sundays. Rehearsals and appearances filled the days left over, and she had almost managed to forget that it wouldn't last forever.

Almost.

Brandon felt her freeze beneath him, and he hesitated, bending back to take in her expression. He saw the pain in her eyes, and he suspected she was thinking about the end of the show again. They hadn't discussed her impending departure since the day he'd told her he was staying in Granbury as the permanent managing director.

They'd both been riding along on the impossible dream that if they didn't discuss the problem, maybe it didn't really exist. He'd promised to give her time to sort out her thoughts. But time was closing in on them.

"What's wrong, Felicia?" he asked, knowing the answer already. Knowing the time had come when they had to face it.

He watched her swallow tightly, her eyes glued to his. She took a deep breath, then sighed as if the weight of the world rested on her.

"You're right, Brandon," she said. "Some things don't ever change. I can't stay in Granbury. That was true eight years ago. And it's still true. I don't know why we keep going on like this, pretending it's not."

She pulled away from him and sat up, hugging her knees to her chest. Brandon sat up, too, sitting close to her, their thighs brushing.

"But there are things that have changed, as well," Brandon countered softly. "Eight years ago, you left without telling me. This time we're talking about it. Eight years ago, you were holding a lot of pain inside, pain that you're beginning to deal with now."

Felicia's eyes darted to his.

"You don't have to be afraid of intimacy," he said gently. "Because I love you doesn't mean I'm going to hurt you. Or that I'll leave you eventually. Love doesn't have to mean pain. You don't have to leave me before I can leave you."

Felicia stared at him, wide-eyed.

"I didn't—" she started.

"You did," Brandon cut in. "I don't think you believe anyone can love you, because of your mother. Because she left you."

Silence, broken only by the sound of the lake slapping softly against the shore, rose between them.

"It's not that simple," Felicia whispered finally.

"I know it's not," he said, taking her hand into his, squeezing his fingers against her palm. "But it's not that complicated, either."

"I have to have my career. It's what validates me as a person," she told him. "I have to make my way on my own. I always have. I don't want to be dependent on anybody else."

Brandon shook his head.

"I don't want you to stay in Granbury and be dependent on me. I'd never ask you to do that."

"Then what are you asking? They don't make movies in Granbury, Brandon."

"No, but the Opera House is here. Taking on the creative direction of it is an exciting challenge. You could share that with me. You could work on the West Coast, yet still keep your hand in the theater here." He stared at her, his eyes serious and dark. "It's not that unusual an idea, having two homes."

"Oh, and this would be my vacation home?"

"I hope you'd consider it more than that. I'd want you to be my equal partner in the guidance of the Opera House."

The thought of how exciting she'd found working at the Opera House in the last weeks flashed into Felicia's mind. The idea of continuing her association with the theater appealed to her. But then, just as quickly, she thought of the separations from Brandon, the uncertainty that would follow. The fear.

"And you'd be here, waiting for me, whenever I wanted to pop into town?" Felicia asked coolly. "It wouldn't work, Brandon. We'd be apart too much. It would eat away at our hearts. You'd turn to—"

"Turn to someone else?" He laughed, a hard edge to the sound. "What does it take to make you believe I love you? Isn't eight years long enough?"

Felicia's eyes flashed up to his.

"You want me to believe you were waiting for me for eight years?" she asked, her voice strained.

She pulled her hand from his, inching her body away so that they no longer touched.

"Of course, there were other women."

Felicia felt a twist of jealousy in her stomach, and frustration stained through her as she recognized it for what it was. She knew she had no right to be jealous of any relationships Brandon might have had during the years they were apart. But feelings didn't have to be reasonable.

"I'm sorry," she said. There was a crack in her voice that she couldn't help. "I don't have any right—"

Brandon grabbed her hands, pulling both of them into his, forcing her to meet his gaze.

"You have every right," he insisted. "You were there, a part of every one of those relationships. You were a ghost, a haunting memory. You invaded every relationship I ever had. I couldn't forget you."

Felicia licked her lips.

"I didn't forget you, either," she admitted. And suddenly the need to tell him about Rodney, to somehow explain, surged within her. "I never forgot you, even when I married Rodney," she whispered.

"Felicia, you don't have to—"

"Yes, I do," she interrupted firmly.

She stared out to the lake for a silent moment. Putting into words why she married Rodney was difficult. Especially to Brandon. But she felt that he of all people had a right to know.

"We were partners, we worked well together. The public seemed to like us together. I was alone. I was afraid." Felicia bit her bottom lip, knowing that though all those reasons were true, they still didn't explain why she'd married him. Quiet stretched between them. "I didn't love him."

Brandon studied her profile, sensing the inward struggle that had taken place as she'd voiced her thoughts to him. Keeping one hand curled over hers, he reached up with the other to lightly stroke the line of her cheek. She turned to him, the moonlight revealing the pain in her green depths.

"That's the real reason you married him, isn't it?"

Brandon asked softly. "You didn't love him, so he couldn't hurt you. Not really."

Felicia didn't answer, but the flicker of acceptance in her eyes told him he was right.

"Haven't I convinced you yet that I'll never hurt you? Don't you know that?"

He placed his arm around her back, and she let her head fall against his broad shoulder. They stared out at the lake together.

"I need you to accept that I love you, Felicia." Brandon snuggled her against him, his own heart bursting with the pain he felt emanating from hers. "We can deal with everything else, with the separation. But you have to stop fighting the intimacy. You have to stop closing yourself off from me."

He needed her to admit that she loved him, too. That he wasn't wrong, that her feelings for him were as real as his feelings for her.

"I need time," she said at last, still huddled in the crook of his arm.

"How much time?" Brandon asked, knowing they didn't have much left.

"I don't know."

Brandon spent the next morning searching through county courthouse records for the owner of their secret hideaway beside the lake. When he found the necessary records and telephoned the retired property owner at his Atlanta home, he didn't tell Felicia.

He still didn't tell her when the offer was accepted and the legal documents signed.

He wanted to wait. He wanted to surprise her with the gesture that to him symbolized the permanence of their love.

* * *

Brandon gave everyone off the Wednesday before the last weekend of *Passion's Pride* to rest before the final round of performances. But resting brought too much thinking with it, and Felicia couldn't bear that. Not right now. Her thoughts were a jumble of confusion and pain.

She kept pushing them away, not willing to deal with the fast-approaching end to her time in Granbury. When Robin asked her to take her to Summer Story Hour at the library, instead of having Libby take her, Felicia agreed readily.

The Granbury library, a few blocks from the town square, was a small stone structure that had changed little in eight years. It was a tiny library, by city standards. Or any standards. But it was a warm and friendly place, and the head librarian herself, Nita Brooks, took time out of her day to read to the children and knew them all by name.

Felicia had stopped by to pick Cara up at the Dunbars' house on the way over, and now she watched with pride as Robin plopped down with Cara amid the crowd of children at the library, talking and laughing easily with the group. Not for the first time since she'd returned to Granbury, it struck Felicia how Robin had seemed to bloom while they'd been here. The small-town atmosphere seemed to agree with her. Robin thrived on the attention of townspeople who remembered her by name. Her friendship with Cara had grown fast and deep. Her fair skin was blushed with color from long hours playing outside.

And above all, Robin lapped up the attention of Brandon and Ted. Her little daughter was clearly hungry for the fatherly attention they gave her.

Felicia furrowed her brow as she watched Robin, seeing her child's hazel eyes glow with anticipation as the librarian opened a book and began to read aloud in an animated voice. Felicia didn't want Robin to be hurt by leaving Granbury. But how could she bounce her daughter back and forth between Granbury and California? What kind of life would that be? Felicia wanted, more than anything, for Robin to have some sense of belonging to a place, to feel part of a place.

If they jumped back and forth, Robin could end up feeling like she belonged in neither place. Confusion knifed through Felicia.

She walked outside, needing to feel the brush of the warm morning air on her cheeks. Meandering aimlessly around the side of the library, she noticed a group of women casually crowding around a picnic table in the grassy park behind the building. Two of the women had babies sitting in little carry seats atop the table.

Felicia recognized them as the mothers of some of the older children inside at the story hour. She guessed this was how they regularly spent their time while their children were being read to. It was a comfortable scene. She could hear their laughter and chatter ringing through the air.

For a moment, she longed to go over to join them. She wondered what it was like to be one of them, to live in Granbury, to center their lives around the loving and caring of their husbands and children. To feel safe and secure enough to do that.

To belong, with such a certainty, to this town and to their mates.

An ache filled her, threading a path from the pit of her stomach to her heart. She couldn't imagine feeling that way.

She flipped around and walked the other way, coming to the sidewalk in front of the library, then back around to the other side of the building. The senior citizens' center filled a historic building, Shugart House, which was set back to the rear of the library, and Felicia remembered her grandmother coming there sometimes to quilt and play cards and talk with her friends. She wandered toward the building, thinking of her grandmother.

Out of the corner of her eye, she noticed a car pull up in the parking lot. An elderly woman emerged from the car, shut the door, and headed toward the senior citizen's center. The sudden sound of hissing and spitting rent the silence of the morning, and two cats, a thin orange one chasing a dark, fluffy one, dashed by in little more than a blur.

Felicia heard at the same time a choked scream and a thud. She turned to see the elderly woman on her side in the parking lot. Felicia rushed to her side.

"Are you okay?" Felicia asked, her breath coming quickly as she knelt beside the woman.

"The cats—I tripped over them—"

The woman's voice was tight with pain, and Felicia could see the fear in her eyes.

"My leg. I'm afraid I broke my leg." The woman started to cry.

Felicia stared at her, then reached down quickly to touch her shoulder softly.

"Don't move. I'll get help," she promised, and ran into Shugart House. The woman at the desk inside the senior citizens' center began dialing before Felicia even had her whole first sentence out of her mouth. Confident that expert assistance was on the way, Felicia turned and ran back out to the parking lot. Several seniors, men and women, hurried after her.

Felicia knelt down by the woman lying prone on the hard asphalt.

"Help's coming. Don't try to move," Felicia said, as the woman tried to shift her position.

"My leg," the woman moaned.

Felicia took her hand and squeezed it.

"You'll be okay," she said. She held the woman's hand tighter and, with her other hand, brushed back the wisps of gray hair that fell across the woman's cheek. "It's going to be okay," she said softly.

The others crowded around then, talking to the woman by name and encouraging her, asking where it hurt and assuring her help was coming. But she wouldn't let go of Felicia's hand, as if Felicia was her lifeline to safety. So Felicia sat there and waited with her until the ambulance came. The emergency workers transferred the woman into the vehicle quickly and efficiently, with as little jarring as possible.

Felicia watched the ambulance disappear in the direction of Granbury General Hospital, feeling suddenly drained. She wondered about the woman, if she had any family in town. She wondered if her grandmother had known her.

She glanced around to the senior citizens who'd come out to the parking lot. They were talking quietly among themselves in hushed, concerned tones. Caught up in their worry for their friend, none of them looked Felicia's way. She thought she recognized some of them as friends of her grandmother's, but she couldn't remember their names and none of them seemed to remember her.

A number of other people had emerged from the senior citizens' center by then, and Felicia heard one woman announcing she was going to call the injured woman's daughter and son-in-law. Felicia turned slowly and headed back toward the library.

A sad feeling enveloped her. She hoped the woman

hadn't been injured too badly. And she was glad she had family and friends to comfort her if she had.

As Felicia approached the library, she noticed the group of mothers had disappeared, and she suspected story time was over by now. Inside, she found the mothers gathering their children together and overheard them making plans to meet for lunch together at Peppermint's.

A hollowed-out core of loneliness expanded inside Felicia as she listened. She forced herself to smile as Robin skipped toward her, holding a book in one hand.

"I had lots of fun, Mommy," Robin announced loudly. "Next week there's going to be a puppet show! Miss Brooks said so."

Next week. The two words resounded painfully in Felicia's mind.

Robin had forgotten that she wouldn't be coming to Summer Story Hour next week. She'd be in California.

Felicia didn't tell Brandon that Noreen had called, or that she'd been given the film role. Inside, she was up and down, her spirits jagging between excitement and depression.

Noreen, at least, was pleased. Everything had gone as the agent had planned. She'd manipulated the press coverage to Felicia's advantage, easily developing the angle of her client's new career image. Felicia had no doubt of Noreen's having a heavy hand in Huberts' appearance at the opening night of the Granbury Opera House. And her strategy had worked. Felicia had the part.

But Felicia hadn't told Brandon yet. Neither had she told him that Bob Combs had called and that the young couple who'd wanted to lease the house now wanted to buy it.

The final performance came, and heaviness thudded through her heart as the curtain fell for the last time. Brandon took her hand and stared at her.

"Come with me tonight," he said, and she knew where he meant to take her.

She knew she had to tell him tonight that she'd gotten the film. She'd tried to tell him the night before, but the beguiling sweetness of Brandon's lovemaking had confused her. Whenever they were together at their secret paradise beside the lake, she seemed unable to think straight.

Even now, she couldn't resist him.

"All right," Felicia told him. "Just give me a few minutes."

She changed, removing her makeup and putting on the shorts and T-shirt she'd worn when she had arrived at the theater earlier in the day. She found Brandon waiting for her outside the theater, leaning against his car, staring at the door. He watched her walk toward him, his eyes absorbing her every step.

The way she moved, the hesitancy in her feet and her eyes, sent a ripple of apprehension through him. It was their last night. She'd asked for time and he'd given it, allowing her the space she seemed to need in spite of his own desire to pull her close and never let go.

He opened the car door for her before getting in himself. They drove quietly, speaking in low tones about the play, some of the other cast members, and the Opera board. They talked of everything except what was on both of their minds. When they arrived beneath the live oak tree, Brandon parked and took the quilt out of the trunk. They unfolded it together and spread it over the grassy ground near the water.

"Brandon—"

"I need you, Felicia," he said in a soft voice, his eyes intense. She stared back at him silently.

His mouth moved over hers, settling firmly on her lips, parting them with a swift, greedy flick of his tongue. Felicia opened to him, responding with the same pained need that she sensed in him.

She snaked her arms around his neck, pulling him down on top of her on the soft quilt. He strayed from her mouth, pelting her face and neck with hungry kisses. She drew his chest tight against her until she could barely breathe, wanting the feel of his nearness.

Then he rolled over to his side so he could lift up her shirt. He buried his face in her chest, inhaling the sweet, spring-blossom fragrance she wore and pleasuring in the smooth creaminess of her breasts. Brandon unhooked her bra and feasted on her rose-tipped fullness until she groaned from the sensuous assault.

"Brandon," she moaned, her voice a breathy whisper in the night.

He moved to push down her shorts and pull them away, then stopped to toss his own off. With skillful hands, he readied her. Then, desire and need bonding, he entered her. Their hearts pounded together, hot passion streaking over them.

Her scent, the wild tumble of her hair, the darkness in her green eyes, all rushed over and through him. The keen ecstasy of having her, the sure knowledge of the fragility of their time together, was almost too much to bear.

He pulsed up and down, and she kept up with him stroke for stroke. She felt giddy from the speed and fervency of his possession, yet didn't draw away from it, didn't try to stop it. He was all fire and need and yearning. And she understood all of those things.

Rapture and wonder filled the final seconds before

they collapsed together against the quilt, limp and boneless. Brandon lay beside her, his breath coming fast, his heart pounding in his chest. Aching.

He reached and found Felicia's hand and squeezed it inside his own. They lay there together without moving for a long time before they finally dressed, then sat down together on the quilt. Felicia leaned against Brandon, fitting smoothly into the sheltering crook of his shoulder.

"Marry me, Felicia," he said into the still night.

She was silent. She hunched her knees up under her chin, staring out at the rippling, shimmering water of Lake Granbury.

"I can't."

"Why not?"

"What kind of marriage could we have?" She turned to stare at him, her eyes wide. He saw an ache there, and he recognized it. He felt it, too.

"The kind of marriage that two people who love each other have," he told her. "Not a perfect one. Nobody has a perfect marriage. But it would be ours, we'd have each other."

"Part-time, you mean," she said, a bitter tinge in her voice. "For as long as it lasts."

"I love you, Felicia. That's not going to change. We wouldn't be the first couple to deal with separation."

He wanted to convince her, to persuade her that everything was possible if they loved each other enough. He wanted to tell her that he'd bought the land, but he held back.

Yet he couldn't stop himself from trying to convince her to stay, ignoring the tiny voice inside that told him she had to decide for herself. He couldn't make her do anything.

"I can't do this to Robin," Felicia argued. "I can't take her back and forth, with no place to call home."

"Stop hiding behind Robin!" Brandon cried out in frustration.

"I'm not hiding," Felicia insisted. "I don't want Robin to feel like I did, that she has no place, no real home. I don't want to jerk her around the country. She's going to start school this fall. She needs stability."

Felicia felt her heart breaking, but she was determined. She'd made up her mind before they ever got in the car to come to their secret place tonight. She'd known when she came that she was coming to say goodbye. She just hadn't realized how shattering the goodbye would be.

But she feared the wrenching pain a series of goodbyes would bring if they tried to stay together, living two thousand miles apart. She would never know which goodbye was the last. She didn't want Robin to see her pain, to grow even more attached to Granbury and Brandon than she already had.

"You're afraid." Brandon's accusation hovered between them, and Felicia didn't dispute it.

She had admitted to herself already that she was afraid. She'd waited to see if the sensation disappeared after being recognized, but it hadn't. It had grown, instead.

Eight years ago, Brandon had asked her to marry him in this same spot. She'd been afraid of losing her heart and soul to him then. She wasn't any less afraid now.

"You don't know that it won't work out," Brandon said. "You're afraid to even try." He sighed heavily and ran his fingers roughly through his chestnut hair.

Felicia sighed, too.

"Noreen called yesterday," she told him suddenly. "I got the part."

Silence met her announcement.

"Filming starts next week. It'll take three months. I can't possibly be back in Granbury until the end of October, if then." She watched him, noticing the coldness that had crept over his features. "Of course, Robin will be in school, so we won't be able to leave then. Maybe we could see you over Christmas holidays."

She shook her head.

"It won't work, Brandon. You're just too stubborn to admit it. I have tickets to fly out to L.A. tomorrow morning. There's no time left to kid ourselves." She stood up. Tears threatened at the edges of her eyes.

Brandon sat, frozen, for a moment. Then he stood beside her. He caught her eyes, noticing the moist pools there. He longed to grab her to him, hold her tight and never let go.

Looking into her eyes, the anger that had risen left him. He felt only pain.

"I guess I should be grateful you took the time to say goodbye this time," he said, forcing a calm he didn't feel into his voice. He stooped to pick up the quilt and made his way slowly back to the car.

The ride home was silent.

ELEVEN

Felicia turned her key in the lock of her spacious California stucco house, which was perched high on a hill overlooking the busy sprawl of Los Angeles. She found Robin in the living room, lazily staring at the television screen, a box of graham crackers beside her. Libby was scrunched up in the corner of the plump white sofa, reading a romance novel. Bright afternoon sunlight poured in through the long back windows.

"Felicia!" Libby tossed the book down casually and stretched. "You're home early."

Felicia smiled slightly, exhaustion tearing at her. The last few months had been difficult and tiring. The film version of *Passion's Pride*, renamed *Price of Passion* at Howard Huberts' whim, was finally completed, at least on Felicia's part.

Getting back into the flow of film work, performing without the stimulation of a live audience, was more difficult than Felicia had expected. She had performed in films for years now, and the lack of immediacy in the work had never bothered her before. But she found it did now, and her mind kept returning to the exhilaration of performing to a crowd as she had at the Granbury Opera House. She missed it, she missed the creative energy of it, the inspiration it offered, the stirring power of the give and take between audience and performer.

And she missed Brandon.

She'd found solace in her role as Veronica but was annoyed by Huberts' insistence on reshaping the character with a more shallow edge than Felicia had given her on the stage in Granbury. She found Veronica less sympathetic in Huberts' version, less likeable, and she disliked her lack of control over the role. Huberts didn't seem to fully appreciate Felicia's efforts to imbue the role with the emotion and depth that she'd given it on the Granbury stage, and the constant conflict over the interpretation of the character had been draining.

Huberts wanted to see the Felicia Marick he'd seen in her prior films. Despite the high marks he'd given the performance that he'd witnessed in Granbury, when filming actually began, he preferred she play the role in a way reminiscent of her past work—with a superficiality of character that no longer satisfied Felicia.

The only change Huberts made that she did like was that Veronica and Stefan reunited in the end, their love winning out. Playing those final reunion scenes was painful for Felicia, as she constantly remembered Brandon's performance as Stefan. But the fantasy of it, the notion of love triumphing over all, was thrilling in a bittersweet way.

Sweet because she could close her eyes and imagine she was saying the words in the script to Brandon, instead of to an actor whom she barely knew. And bitter because she'd found out only too sharply, too recently, that love didn't conquer all.

Felicia plopped onto the soft couch beside Libby and put her feet up on the smooth, polished coffee table. Robin jumped up and crawled onto the sofa beside her mother.

"How was school today?" Felicia asked, ruffling Robin's curly locks.

Felicia felt she'd missed so much these last few months. Busy and tired, Robin's first couple of months of kindergarten had sped by for Felicia. Some nights she'd come in too late to have even a chance to talk to Robin before she went to bed.

The situation had gotten so bad that one morning Robin had complained of severe stomach cramps and refused to go to school. The little girl had gotten nearly hysterical when Felicia tried to leave for work, with instructions for Libby to take Robin in to see the doctor. Felicia had finally called in to the set and taken off work, leaving a film crew hanging for half a day while she rushed a tearful Robin to the doctor. She'd worried herself half sick only to discover that Robin was perfectly fine and had pretended to be ill in order to get her mother's attention.

After that unsettling episode, Felicia had tried to balance her work and home life more carefully, but the results had been uneven at best. Stress and guilt had plagued Felicia. She knew she wasn't giving her best to either part of her life.

"School was okay," Robin said, the same bored tone in her voice that she always used when she was asked about school.

Felicia knew Robin missed Cara and her other little friends her age that she'd met through the story time at the Granbury library. But she'd hoped Robin would meet new friends when she started kindergarten. It worried Felicia that her daughter appeared so uninterested in any of the children at her school.

"Can we go to the store now, Mommy?" Robin asked, touching her mother's arm and staring up at her hopefully.

Felicia crinkled her forehead.

"You said you'd take me to get a costume for Halloween today if you got to come home early," Robin reminded her, a fitful whine entering her voice.

Felicia remembered then. Her tired bones rejected the prospect of tramping through a department-store costume section, waiting patiently while Robin chose a Halloween outfit. But she'd promised.

"Sure," Felicia agreed, forcing brightness into her words.

"Felicia?"

Libby was staring at her, an odd, unreadable expression in her eyes.

"I have to talk to you," she said. Her voice sounded strangely serious for Libby.

"Okay," Felicia said, wondering what Libby could possibly need to talk to her about that could be so serious.

"Not here," Libby said, glancing at Robin, then back to Felicia. "Maybe in the kitchen."

Now Felicia was even more curious.

"All right," she said, standing. "You stay here, sweetie," she told Robin. The little girl stretched out on the sofa, chin on fists, and stared at the television.

"What is it?" Felicia asked as soon as she and Libby were in the long, light, modern kitchen.

European-style cabinets and a gleaming white tiled floor lent a crisp, clean atmosphere to the room. Felicia didn't cook, and Libby rarely delved into anything more complex than sandwiches and chocolate-chip cookies, so the kitchen was always immaculate. They ate out a lot, or brought home take-out. Not the most healthy way to live, Felicia suspected, but she and Libby both preferred the ease of it.

Libby spent her time seeing to Robin, as well as managing passably well at housecleaning, so Felicia didn't press her to cook. Felicia had almost hired a housekeeper to cook and clean once, but she had backed out at the last minute. Her hard-working country roots had rebelled at the notion of hiring someone simply to cook for her. It was too silly, she'd decided.

And so the kitchen was awfully clean an awful lot of the time.

Felicia sat down at the sparkling clean glass-topped kitchen table, the hazy afternoon sun streaming over it, and stared at Libby expectantly. Libby sat down across from her and hesitated as she fingered the edges of the blue-and-white-striped placemat in front of her. Her eyes scooted from Felicia's, avoiding meeting her gaze.

"Libby? Come on. What's wrong?" Felicia demanded, growing more worried the longer Libby was silent. It wasn't like her not to come right out and say whatever was on her mind.

Libby looked up finally, biting her lower lip nervously. "Well, I guess I might as well just tell you," she started.

"Please do."

"I'm leaving."

"What? " Felicia stared at her, aghast. Libby couldn't leave them. She just couldn't! "What are you talking about?"

"I'm going back to Granbury." Libby's eyes moistened. Felicia could see that the words came hard from her, but her voice resounded with determination. "I don't want to leave you, Felicia. And I've been with

Robin since the day you brought her home from the hospital. This is so hard. I can hardly stand it."

"What do you mean you're going back to Granbury?" Felicia asked, floored. She knew Libby had taken it rough when they'd left Granbury, just as Robin had. Libby had continued her relationship with Ted Jarvis, with weekly letters and daily telephone calls.

But to go back to Granbury?

"Libby, are you sure? You can't have thought this through." Felicia shook her head.

"I have, Felicia. It's all I've thought of," Libby told her. "Ever since Ted asked me to marry him."

"He asked you to marry him?" Felicia had no idea their relationship had become so serious.

"Last week."

"You've only thought about this a week? Libby! You don't know what you're doing. You hardly know Ted."

"I know that I'm in love with him, and that he loves me," Libby insisted. "I know that he's already rented us a little two-bedroom house near the square. And I know that we're going to get married by the justice of the peace in the gazebo on the courthouse lawn. It's still warm in Georgia at the beginning of November." A tear glistened in her eyes, then fell, streaking a path down her cheek. "It's going to be so beautiful."

Felicia felt tears spring to her own eyes as she listened. She realized she'd never seen Libby in love before.

"Oh, Libby, I want you to be happy," Felicia said, a catch in her voice. She went around the table and leaned down to hug her, and they cried together as they embraced. Felicia drew back a moment later, and they both laughed a little as they swiped at their faces with the backs of their hands. Felicia sat down again, reaching for one of the paper napkins from the brass holder in the middle of the table.

"Do you understand?" Libby asked. "I want you to give me your blessing. I don't want you to be mad at me for leaving you."

Felicia shook her head.

"I'm not mad, I promise," she said. "As long as you're sure. . . ."

"I'm sure," Libby said staunchly. She narrowed her eyes, then, and shot Felicia a sharp glance. "I'm worried about you, Felicia. You'll be here all by yourself, just you and Robin. I know you're not happy."

"I'm happy," Felicia countered, but she didn't sound convincing, even to herself.

Libby pursed her lips and crossed her arms.

"You haven't been the same since we came back from Granbury," she said. "You miss Brandon. I know you do. I don't understand what happened with you two. You're perfect for each other. He loves you. I know it."

Felicia felt the old, familiar pain fill her. Yes, she missed Brandon. She missed him every day, every night, with an ache that never left her. But what could she do about it? Her life was here. She had a career here, a life that held meaning for her.

She closed her eyes tightly for a second, feeling the hollowness of her excuses. In the past few months, she'd found less and less satisfaction in her film work. She had no control, no creative power. It had been different on the stage at the Granbury Opera House. Those few short weeks of thrilling creativity had spoiled her. Brandon's love had spoiled her. Nothing else held meaning.

Felicia flashed her eyes open and met Libby's questioning gaze.

"I can't explain," she said softly, averting her gaze from Libby's curious interest. "Things change, people change. You can't ever go back to the past. Not really."

Libby furrowed her brow.

"Look, I don't know what you mean, or what happened with you guys. But you can work it out if you really want to, Felicia," she said firmly. "Look at me. I'm marrying Ted."

"You're different."

"How? Brandon loves you, Felicia, just like Ted loves me." Libby shook her head. "A few months won't have changed that."

"There's more to it than that," Felicia explained. "There's my work. And there's Robin to consider."

"Robin wants to go back to Granbury more than anything else!" Libby cried. "Just ask her. All she does is moan and groan about Granbury."

"I couldn't take her out of school," Felicia said.

Libby frowned.

"What's the real problem, Felicia? Robin wants to go. She'd adjust to a new school. She already has friends in Granbury." Libby shifted in her seat, leaning forward onto the table. "And you're not happy with your work here anymore. I've seen how tired and strained you are. You've lost weight. You're nervous."

Felicia knew everything Libby was saying was true, and more. Libby didn't know about all the sleepless nights, about the days she had dragged herself into the studio when she'd wanted to cry at home, instead. Not to mention the guilt she felt over Robin's obvious unhappiness.

But she couldn't go back to Granbury. Not after what she'd said to Brandon. She'd told him they had no future. She'd insisted she couldn't stay in Granbury.

And he'd let her go. She hadn't heard a word from him since she had come back. No doubt he'd gone on with his life by now. He wouldn't want to see her. It was too late to change her mind.

And she'd sold her grandmother's house to the young couple the Realtor had found. She'd agreed to the sale a few weeks after she'd returned to L.A., believing that with the house gone she'd be able to close that chapter on her life for good. She'd instructed Bob Combs to see to the packing and storage of the furniture and personal items in the house, and she had signed the formal papers.

But she hadn't closed the book. Brandon's eyes haunted her every night as she lay in the lonely oak bed in her room with its wide windows overlooking the impersonal spread of the city below.

"I can't go back," Felicia whispered.

Libby was silent a moment.

"Well, Ted and I are getting married on the courthouse lawn at eleven o'clock in the morning next Saturday," Libby told her. "I'd love it if you'd come."

Felicia stared across the table at her.

"I don't think I could do that," she said.

"Think about it, that's all," Libby said. "Now, I've got to go talk to Robin, I guess. I hate to tell her I'm leaving. Maybe you guys should go shopping for her Halloween costume first, then we'll tell her together when you get back. My plane leaves tomorrow morning. I only waited to be sure you'd finished filming. I've already started packing. I'm so excited, Felicia!"

Libby stood up, and Felicia rose and hugged her again. Then they turned together toward the living room. Felicia stopped Libby suddenly, before they left the kitchen, with a soft brush of her hand against Libby's shoulder. Libby turned and stared at her.

"Libby, aren't you scared?" Felicia asked, her voice low. "How can you just up and go out there? You haven't known Ted that long. Aren't you afraid it won't work out?"

Felicia's green eyes met Libby's dark, serious gaze. Libby's expression softened, and she smiled gently.

"No, I'm not afraid," Libby told her, confidence glowing in her eyes. "Relationships don't come with money-back guarantees, Felicia. You just have to believe in love." She shook her head, her red wavy locks bouncing over her shoulders. "If you're not willing to take any chances in life—especially for the things that really count, like love—you might as well be dead. You know?"

Brandon glanced up from his desk, alerted by the knock on his office door. Ted slouched against the doorjamb, twisting his lips around. He'd been acting jumpy as a cat for weeks, and the intense expression on his face gave Brandon the idea he was about to find out why.

"What's up, Ted?" he asked, struggling to focus his attention on the young actor and away from the drifting, distant thoughts of Felicia that had haunted him since she'd left.

Sitting at his desk, staring at the lumpy orange chair across from him, Brandon had been remembering the way Felicia had looked that first day she'd come into the Opera House. Sexy, fresh, and more beautiful than he'd ever seen her, with her long wheat-gold hair swinging down her back, the soft lines of her flower-patterned sundress flattering the curves of her body.

It was an image that haunted him relentlessly. He kept wondering if he could have done things differently, if he could have somehow convinced her to stay.

But the saner side of him knew he'd done all he could. She'd made her decision, and he had to live with it.

"I've been wanting to ask you something," Ted said as he sauntered in and slung down into the chair across from Brandon's desk.

Brandon forced a pleasant smile, recalling himself sharply to reality. It was time he quit thinking about Felicia, he chastised himself. Months had passed. She hadn't come back, she hadn't called.

She hadn't changed her mind. Even her grandmother's house was sold now. She'd made it as clear as she possibly could that she was through with Granbury, and Brandon, for good this time.

And it was high time he accepted it. He'd begun considering selling the lake lot. Their lake lot, where he'd dreamed they'd build their own home someday. Brandon had picked up the phone to dial a Realtor at least half a dozen times, and every time he'd put the phone back down.

"What can I do for you?" Brandon asked heartily, turning his thoughts to the matter at hand. The company had just completed a rousing rendition of Shakespeare's *A Midsummer Night's Dream*, in which Ted had enjoyed high accolades for his portrayal of the mischievous Puck.

The management and direction of the historic Granbury Opera House had been as challenging and creatively fulfilling as Brandon had suspected when he'd first become interested in the position. He enjoyed overseeing the theater's creative direction, relished the opportunity to select at will his own parts in the shows—and savored as well the choice to simply remain behind the scenes in some productions.

But his heart sometimes felt numb when he thought

of how much he would have delighted in sharing the guidance of the Opera House with Felicia, with her talent and creative ability at his side. But she'd insisted that her future was in California, and he wouldn't have her give up her career dreams for his. He'd hoped once that there could be some kind of compromise, but he knew now that it wasn't going to happen.

At least, he knew it intellectually. Convincing his heart was yet another matter.

"I want you to be my best man," Ted said, interrupting Brandon's thoughts.

"What?"

"I'm getting married this Saturday," Ted said, a sheepish grin stealing across his features. "I asked Libby, and she accepted. She's flying out today. In fact, I'm about to leave for the airport. I've been wanting to ask you for a couple of days, but I waited to be sure Libby was going to be able to make it this week. She wouldn't leave Felicia until she was finished with her movie. She didn't want to leave Robin when Felicia was in the middle of a project."

So Felicia had finished the movie, Brandon thought. He wondered how things had gone, if she was happy.

Then a thought struck him.

"Are Felicia and Robin coming out with Libby? Are they coming to the wedding?"

"Libby's coming alone," Ted said, shaking his head.

The sudden hope was doused instantly. Brandon took a deep breath.

"Congratulations," he said, standing and stretching his hand across the desk. Ted smiled as they shook hands.

"Saturday morning, eleven o'clock." Ted looked at Brandon hopefully. "In the gazebo by the courthouse."

"Sure. I'll be there. Wouldn't miss it," Brandon told him, forcing a reciprocal smile.

"Great."

Ted bounded out of the room, whistling cheerily. Brandon sat back down behind his desk, his appetite for the work in front of him vanished. He was happy for Ted, but he couldn't help thinking that it could have been Felicia and him in the courthouse gazebo, exchanging vows and promises of forever.

He shook his head slowly. There was certainly no sense wasting time thinking about could-have-beens. Reaching for the thin Granbury phone book, he flipped through until he put his finger on the number he needed.

"Bob Combs Realty," came the clipped, business-like voice of the receptionist.

Halloween was a disaster. Robin was distressed over Libby's departure, and even donning the dainty ballerina costume she'd chosen did little to brighten her spirits. Felicia took her to all the houses on the streets surrounding their home. But Felicia didn't know any of her neighbors, so afterward she felt compelled to take Robin downtown to the hospital, where they'd waited for an hour among a rowdy bunch of howling children to have Robin's candy X-rayed.

By the time they'd gotten home, Robin had been too tired to eat more than two pieces of her safety-checked loot before she'd fallen asleep on the living room floor. Felicia carried Robin to her room, then wandered into the kitchen tiredly in search of sustenance herself.

A container of the remnants of Libby's last batch of chocolate-chip cookies met her eyes first, so she grabbed a handful and settled down at the glass-topped kitchen table with a cup of water and flipped through a stack of unopened mail. At the bottom of the sprawl of mail, she noticed a large manila envelope and pulled it out. The return address was Granbury—Lola Dunbar.

Felicia took a sip of water and opened the clasp. Reaching inside the envelope, she withdrew a thick pile of newspaper clippings and a short, typewritten letter.

She scanned the letter quickly. In it, Lola apologized for not writing sooner. She expressed her formal appreciation on behalf of the Opera board for Felicia's generous support of the Opera House reopening, mentioning as well that the Opera House was continuing successfully under Brandon's management. Lola ended by noting that the clippings enclosed represented a compilation of all the publicity generated by the Opera House reopening, which she thought Felicia might be interested in having.

A tightness around her chest nearly choked Felicia as she unfolded the first clipping. It was the *Granbury Globe* article showing Brandon and Felicia at the podium the night of the Opera House Ball.

The night Brandon had kissed her and moved her heart and soul with the sweet power of his seduction. A wave of longing rolled over Felicia.

She placed the paper facedown on the kitchen table and flipped through the remaining clippings, unsure of whether or not she really wanted to look at them all.

Unsure of whether she could bear to.

She came to the last clipping, a short article dealing with the overwhelming response of new and former financial backers who'd joined in to reopen the Opera House. The front-page article was written soon after Felicia had left Granbury. Interested, she read through the entire piece, pleased to see the abundance that their benefit production had brought. The financial backing had poured in, both locally and state-wide, in response to the high level of publicity that Brandon and Felicia's involvement had prompted.

She put the clipping down, glad that something good had come of her trip to Granbury. Something more than heartache.

The back of the clipping revealed part of the newspaper opinion page, and Felicia stared at it idly. Her eyes widened at the words she read.

To the Editor,

Recently, I injured myself outside Shugart House. A nice young woman, whose name I didn't have the presence of mind at the time to get, helped me. I hope she'll read this letter and know how much her kind attention meant to me. She didn't know me, but she stayed by my side until the ambulance came, holding my hand. That's the sort of neighborly love that makes Granbury the place it is—a warm and wonderful town to live in. Thank you again, neighbor. By the way, I'm doing better now.
Signed,

Celia Dewey
Granbury

Felicia stared at the paper. Memories of Granbury washed over her. Not the memories of her childhood, tainted by her mother's abandonment, when Felicia had felt unwanted and unloved. She'd thought she didn't belong in Granbury because her mother hadn't belonged there, because her mother didn't want her.

Instead, Felicia's mind traveled to memories of the reality of the Granbury she and Robin had experienced during the past summer, the Granbury that had opened its arms and hearts to them both. The Granbury that didn't ponder Felicia's past, but simply assumed she belonged and treated her like a native daughter.

Felicia recalled the day she'd taken Robin to the library and how left out she'd felt that day. Looking back, she could see that she should have gone over and talked to the other mothers sitting at the picnic table. Maybe they'd been afraid to approach her, knowing who she was.

And she could have asked the seniors outside Shugart House if they'd known her grandmother. Thinking back on the incident, Felicia realized it was she who had held herself apart and separate.

Just as she'd held herself apart and separate from Brandon, always afraid to take that extra step that might open herself to rejection. Always shielding her heart from the vulnerability that came with risk.

Felicia stared down at the stack of newspaper clippings that told of Granbury's warm acceptance of her return. The town had accepted her. Brandon had accepted her. Everyone had offered her love and acceptance, the kind of belonging she'd yearned for all her life.

And she'd turned her back on it all. For the second time.

Felicia looked around at the immaculate, pristine cleanliness of her kitchen. Images of Granbury flashed into her mind. Brandon helping her make coffee that first morning after he'd fished her out of Lake Granbury when her canoe had overturned. Brandon offering her coffee and telling her she was beautiful the night she'd fallen asleep in his arms at his house. Brandon making slow, sweet love to her by the shore of the lake.

Then her mind turned to their last night, when he'd

asked her to marry him, there in the same spot where he'd proposed to her eight years before.

And she'd left him, replaying the pain of their past. Felicia squeezed her eyes shut, wishing she could block out the memory of how she'd hurt him, how she'd hurt herself.

Then she remembered Libby's wedding plans. *If you're not willing to take chances in life, you might as well be dead.*

Felicia's eyes flicked open. She stared at the blackness of night outside the window. She stood and crossed the room to the pantry. Opening the long cabinet door, she peered in, picking up the heavy local phone book.

Her fingers shook as she dialed the number.

TWELVE

Felicia stood, Robin's small hand encased in hers, in the shade of the gazebo on the lawn outside the century-old limestone courthouse. The air was crisp, tinged with the fresh fragrance of fall. The light noise of traffic around Granbury's town square carried on the soft breeze, wrapping the group of wedding attendees with the hum of activity and life of the small town.

The sounds of her hometown.

The ceremony hadn't started yet. The justice of the peace was late.

And so was Brandon.

Felicia knew he was coming because as soon as Libby had spotted her and Robin striding across the square toward the gazebo, she'd run to them, laughing with joy that they'd come after all and bursting to tell Felicia that Brandon would be there as well. Libby, exhibiting all her normal exuberance, displayed no care for the lace-and-ribbon-edged white gown that fluttered around her as she ran across the grass, throwing her arms enthusiastically around Robin. Then she hugged Felicia, chattering happily about Brandon.

But he hadn't shown up yet, and it was nearly eleven o'clock. Dory was there with Cara. Robin and Cara had been thrilled to see each other, and plans for a sleep-over at the Dunbars' house that night were already in progress.

Felicia and Robin had arrived late the night before and had settled into one of the comfortable rooms at the historic Springwater Hotel on the town square. Felicia had decided not to call Libby, due to the lateness of the hour, and so they'd ended up surprising her instead when they showed up at the gazebo.

A small crowd had already gathered by the time Felicia and Robin had arrived, including several Opera House company members. A middle-aged couple who Felicia recognized as Libby's parents hovered about the bride, the woman fussing sporadically with Libby's hair and dress. Another older couple waited quietly, and Felicia suspected they were Ted's parents.

"There he is," Dory cried.

Felicia turned, her stomach churning with nervous anticipation. A short, round man who looked to be in his early sixties, his bald head shining in the morning sun, approached across the clipped grass. She guessed he was the justice of the peace.

"What about Brandon?" one of the actors asked.

"Maybe he's not coming," someone else put in.

"Oh, he has to," Libby said, whirling toward them, her eyes round. "We can't start the wedding without him. He has the ring!"

Felicia looked down, feeling the tug on her hand. Robin was getting antsy with waiting, crowded as they were in the gazebo.

"Let's go take a turn around the courthouse," Felicia whispered, bending down to Robin's ear. Her daughter skipped gleefully beside her as they walked down the gazebo steps and across the lawn. They wandered through the shade of the leafy trees as they trailed around the courthouse. Robin stopped to pick up a few of the oval-shaped, hard brown nuts that lay scattered in the grass.

"What are these, Mommy?" Robin asked.

"Pecans," Felicia answered, her mind clicking ahead nervously. Where was Brandon? she wondered. What would he think when he saw her? Would he be glad she was here? Was it too late for them?

Felicia glanced up at the courthouse clock. It read eleven o'clock precisely.

Brandon hurried out through the tall doors of the Granbury Opera House. He'd been about to leave for Ted and Libby's wedding when a call had come into his office from a potential backer for the Opera House, and it had taken him nearly twenty minutes to get off the phone politely.

Glancing up at the courthouse clock, he saw that it was only a few minutes past eleven. He breathed a sigh of relief and felt in his pocket automatically to reassure himself that he had the ring Ted had entrusted him with earlier in the day. He stepped up to the curb, preparing to cross the street and hurry to the gazebo. He looked out across the square, and his breath froze in his throat.

A woman, long golden hair flowing down her back, strolled across the green lawn, holding hands with an energetic young girl. The child skipped and hopped, hands tightly clasped with her mother's, her bright yellow dress fanning out around her. The woman wore a softly clinging blue dress that revealed, even across the square, the firmness of her curves, the sensuality of her stride.

Brandon blinked, then looked again.

The woman was still there. She wasn't a dream.

Barely remembering to check the traffic before he moved into the street, he crossed the square, his eyes glued to the pair on the courthouse lawn. They had begun moving back toward the gazebo and the wedding party that waited there.

Brandon approached the gazebo, his heart twisting inside his chest. Felicia and Robin had reached the wedding party and held their backs to him. He quickly mounted the few steps to the shade of the gazebo's interior.

"Brandon!" Libby cried, then sighed loudly. "Thank goodness you're here."

Felicia turned. Her eyes met Brandon's, her misty emerald depths filled with anxiety and question. An almost tangible sparkle of electricity passed between them.

Brandon met her gaze coolly, uncertainty filling him now that he faced her. When he first saw her, walking in front of the courthouse, he'd wanted to run up to her, grab her and whirl her around with joy.

But he didn't know why she'd come. Not really. She could have come just for the wedding, he reminded himself.

Neither had a chance to speak before the briefly delayed wedding began.

With everyone assembled, the justice of the peace embarked on the ceremony. In his slow, country drawl, the county official repeated the wedding vows, patiently turning to Ted and Libby in turn for their individual recitations of promise and love.

Libby's eyes shone with happiness, and Ted, for his part, glowed with obvious adoration. Observing the simplicity of their dedication to each other, Felicia felt tears spring to her eyes as they vowed to love, honor, and cherish each other for the rest of their lives.

At the appropriate moment, Ted turned to Brandon for the ring. Brandon fumbled in his pocket before handing the symbol of eternal love to the groom.

Felicia watched Brandon, thinking over and over of the moment a few months ago when he'd asked her to marry him. He looked up at her, his expression unreadable, and she wondered if he was thinking about it, too.

Suddenly, Felicia realized Ted and Libby were kissing, everyone else was applauding, and the wedding was completed. A barbecue and picnic at Ted and Libby's house was planned in celebration of the ceremony. Some in the gathering decided to walk the few short blocks to the couple's new home, while others opted to drive. Robin eagerly asked to walk with Cara and Dory, and then skipped away gladly when Felicia gave her assent.

The gazebo quickly emptied until Felicia stood under the shade of its roof with only Brandon. He lazed casually with his shoulder resting against a post. His gaze rested on her with a languid attention, as if he was in no hurry. As if he knew that, sooner or later, she would come to him.

"Hello, Brandon," she said softly, moving across the gazebo toward him. She stopped a pace away. Holding out her hand seemed ridiculously formal. A hug was painfully impossible.

"Hello, Felicia."

He didn't move, but remained staring at her. Waiting.

Felicia's throat felt dry, and her stomach was churning. He wasn't going to make it easy for her, she decided. But then, she hadn't expected him to. He'd asked her to marry him twice, and she'd refused him twice.

She had no right to expect anything at all.

"They'll be very happy, I'm sure," Felicia said, stalling. "Libby and Ted, I mean."

Brandon nodded.

"How are you?" she asked, searching his face, his eyes, aching for any sign that he was glad to see her. But his expression was impassive, his eyes cool.

He straightened and gave her a crooked half smile.

"I'm fine," he said, his voice gentle. "What about you?"

Felicia grinned ruefully, relieved to feel a break in the ice between them.

"Okay," she answered. She hesitated, then plunged forward. "I guess I've missed . . . Granbury."

"Granbury?"

Felicia pursed her lips. The familiar tingle of fear threaded through her. She took a deep breath. Consequences be damned, she was going to do what she'd come to do.

She had to find out if Brandon still wanted her.

"I missed you." The words were out, and a huge swell of relief rolled over her.

Brandon's eyes narrowed. He saw her nervousness, her hesitation. He felt the tiny ember of hope that he'd nursed these last months ignite inside him.

This time when he smiled, it was a grin that ran from ear to ear. He only just restrained himself from taking her against him right then.

She smiled back, and her deep green eyes sparkled. He couldn't stop himself any longer. He had to touch her. Taking her hand tenderly within his own, he stroked her palm.

"Is that why you came back?" Brandon asked, catching her eyes in his again. He held her gaze softly, watching every flicker of movement in her face.

"Yes," she whispered.

"Because you missed me?"

She swallowed, turning her eyes away. Then she felt a firm touch on her chin, and Brandon brought her face to meet his.

"Because I love you," Felicia admitted, moisture leaping to her eyes.

The silence between them stretched so long, Felicia began to think she'd made a mistake, that jumping in and declaring her feelings had been all wrong. She should have built up to it, should have felt him out a bit first. . . .

Then, with a flash of movement so fast that she didn't even see him coming, Brandon slipped his arm around her waist. He took her snug against his chest and whirled her around, her feet flying from the cement floor of the gazebo.

She laughed with surprise, and he laughed with her, bringing their impetuous dance to a halt. He breathed quickly, his finely planed face lit with happiness as he stared down at her. His sapphire eyes twinkled merrily.

"I love you, Felicia."

"I was so afraid it was too late," she said, sobering as she remembered the fears she'd lived with on her way back to Granbury and up until just a few moments before. "You still . . . love me?"

Brandon shook his head.

"If I haven't convinced you yet, I don't know what—" He stopped suddenly, then slipped his hand into hers again. "Come with me."

He nearly dragged her down the steps from the gazebo and across the square to his car.

"Where are we going? Are we going to Ted and Libby's? They'll probably be wondering where we are." Felicia kept up a steady flow of comments and questions as Brandon keyed the ignition. He turned the car in the opposite direction of Ted and Libby's house.

Within moments, the car slid to a halt in a clearing near the lake. Their clearing. Their place.

Felicia gazed at Brandon, questioning with her eyes. Brandon smiled but said nothing. He rose instead and came around the side of the car to open her door and help her out. They walked hand in hand, quietly, to the shore. The water glittered in the midday sun. Birds swayed overhead. The earth smelled crisp and fresh.

Brandon tugged Felicia's hand, urging her down beside him as he sat. She kicked off her shoes and settled beside him, tucking her dress beneath her thighs. She leaned into Brandon's broad shoulder as she stretched her legs out in front of her.

"I'm sorry," she said softly, watching the gentle roll of the lake. Then she turned up to face him. "I didn't want to leave you, to end it like that." She hesitated for a long moment, then added quickly, "I was afraid."

Brandon sensed, from the strain in her voice, what it cost her to admit that vulnerability. He wrapped his arm around her slim waist and squeezed her against him.

"I'll never stop loving you, Felicia," he promised, his voice low.

"I know," she said. She ran her tongue over her dry lips. Nervousness still reigned inside. She didn't know how to get around to what she really wanted to tell him—that she was ready for marriage. Finally. She was afraid he wouldn't want that now. Not yet.

"What about your work?" Brandon asked suddenly. "Are you content now for us to have a long-distance relationship?"

Felicia shook her head vigorously.

"No. Absolutely not." She grinned wickedly at

Brandon's bemused expression, then she relented and laughed.

"What do you mean?" he asked.

"I want to be here with you in Granbury. I want to work at the Opera House with you." She turned serious. "If you'll have me, of course."

Felicia felt his shoulders shaking before she heard the laughter coming from him.

"If I'll have you," he repeated, rolling his eyes comically. Then he twisted his lips together. "But I don't understand. Your career is important to you. I don't want you to give up your dreams to be near me. I don't want—"

Felicia stopped the flow of words with a touch of her index finger to his smooth lips.

"When I came back here this summer and performed at the Opera House again, I discovered what I'd been missing all these years." She cocked her head to the side, trying to figure out how best to explain how she felt. "This is real. I can see and touch people here. My heart is here." She shrugged. "I called my agent before I left and told her what I'd decided. After Noreen peeled herself off the ceiling, we discussed the possibility of my only taking on carefully selected film projects in the future. I'll probably keep my house out there. I'll continue to work in films. But I want my primary focus to be on the Opera House."

"As long as you aren't giving up anything—"

"Giving up? I'm not giving up anything, Brandon." She shifted toward him, placing her hand in his and smiling into his eyes. "I'm giving up nothing to gain everything. Robin can grow up in a clean, safe place. I can work in a wonderful, vibrant theater while still keeping my contacts on the West Coast. I can take on special projects, films that I really want."

"A few months ago you didn't think any of this was possible," Brandon countered, needing reassurance that she'd thought it all through. It was what he'd wanted to hear her say for so long. But he had to be sure. He couldn't bear it if he lost her again.

"A few months ago I was still letting my fears get in the way of my heart," Felicia told him softly, running a slim finger along the line of his jaw.

Trembles of hot desire shot through Brandon at the sultry trail of her touch on his skin.

"And now?" The words came out as a cracked whisper.

"Now I don't want to be afraid anymore. I had to come back and tell you that I love you. And find out whether or not you still love me." She studied his expression, looking for any sign of uncertainty. What she saw in his face was steady calm. And love.

"I can't stop loving you, Felicia," he said, shaking his head. "Do you remember the day you told me you were afraid this place would be covered with condos?"

Felicia nodded.

"Soon after that, I did a little work at the courthouse and found out who owned this place. I made an offer on six acres."

"You own this place? Our place?" Her eyes widened.

"I almost sold it this week," Brandon told her. "But I just couldn't. I got so far as to call the Realtor. Then I ended up telling him I'd changed my mind halfway through the conversation."

"Why?" Felicia waited for his answer, unconsciously holding her breath.

Brandon reached up to smooth his fingers over the curling blond locks that fell forward over her shoulder. Then he touched the skin of her neck, her throat, and leaned close to press his lips softly over hers.

"I love you too much to give up," he said, his mouth turning upward slightly at the corners. "When I bought it, it was with the dream that we'd build a house here and live here together. Forever."

Forever. The word resounded with love and comfort and commitment.

"Brandon." She said his name in a low voice, catching his eyes, holding them. She moved and clasped both her hands over his large ones. "Will you marry me?"

She waited for his answer, her pulse pounding. He stared at her, his eyes dark and serious. Then he looked away, out to the lake.

"I don't know," he said at last, slowly.

Felicia's heart sank.

"I'm just not sure," Brandon continued, his eyes still averted from hers. "I don't know what to say." He shook his head.

"You don't have to say anything now," Felicia said quickly, fearing already that she'd gone too far, too fast. She'd just come back to town. She shouldn't have asked him this yet. It was wrong, she thought, to assume he was ready just because she finally was. "I'm sorry. I shouldn't have . . ." The words trailed away into an awkward silence.

Brandon heaved a great sigh.

"The problem is this." He turned his gaze to her, facing her squarely. "What if we're not sexually compatible?"

His sapphire eyes twinkled.

"You're teasing me!" she accused, slapping him playfully on the arm. Relief flooded her.

"Yes, I am," he answered, grinning. Then he feigned a glare. "You're not supposed to steal my thunder like that."

"What do you mean?"

"Proposing is my thing. Remember?"

"Oh. That's right. But you haven't been very successful. I thought I'd better do it this time."

"What if I try one more time?"

Felicia hesitated, then smiled flirtatiously, sending ripples of anticipation through Brandon's veins.

"Well, okay. One more time."

Brandon moistened his lips, as if suddenly nervous himself, then touched her face softly, tenderly loving every curve and plane of her features. He kissed her gently, then drew back.

"Felicia, I love you. Will you marry me?"

"Yes."

Brandon threw his arms around her neck in enthusiastic abandon and pulled her to him. They fell backward onto the cool ground, laughing and kissing.

"Did you really say yes?"

"I said yes."

"Say it again."

"Yes!" Felicia shouted.

Brandon covered her mouth with his, whirling his tongue inside her, his need clear in the frenzy of his movements. Then he pulled free, rolling Felicia over beside him. He smiled. He raised his brows suggestively.

"What would you say if I told you I still had that quilt in my trunk?" he asked, his voice thick with passion for her.

"It's light outside!" Felicia protested, looking around at the clearing and the lake, then up at the sky as if she expected a helicopter to be hovering overhead watching them.

"Okay. Wanna go to my house, honey?" he invited, quick to accommodate a change in venue.

"Yes," she answered immediately.

"Are you going to say yes to everything from now on?" he asked.

"Yes," she teased.

He gathered her against him.

"I think I like that," he said.

"I thought you would."

He kissed her, and it was a while before they made it back to the car and drove to his house. It was even longer before they got to the wedding celebration.